While I dozed, I had a dream. All my friends from Room 26 were coming up to my cage and introducing me to their family members. Of course, because I spend each weekend at a different student's house, I knew most of them.

"Humphrey, here's my mom," they said. Or "Humphrey, this is my dad."

I met everybody in my dream from brothers and sisters to aunts and uncles and grandparents of all shapes and sizes. Humans have so many relatives, I don't know how they keep them all straight! And each family is different in a special way.

When I woke up, I had a funny feeling. Where were my mom and dad, my sisters and brothers? Did I have aunts and uncles and cousins?

As far as I could tell, all I had were my human friends and Og the Frog. I consider him a good friend, but I'm pretty sure we're not related. We certainly don't look alike.

I have beautiful golden fur. He is green and has no fur at all. How does he stay warm?

I have a tiny mouth and tiny eyes. Og's eyes are HUGE and so is his mouth.

I say, "SQUEAK."

He says, "BOING!"

No, we're definitely not related.

READ ALL OF HUMPHREY'S ADVENTURES!

NONFICTION BOOKS
FEATURING HUMPHREY

HUMPHREY'S TINY TALES
FOR YOUNG READERS

Spring according to Humphrey

Betty G. Birney

PUFFIN BOOKS

PUFFIN BOOKS
An imprint of Penguin Random House LLC
375 Hudson Street
New York, New York 10014

First published in the United States of America by G. P. Putnam's Sons,
an imprint of Penguin Random House LLC, 2016
Published by Puffin Books, an imprint of Penguin Random House LLC, 2017

THE LIBRARY OF CONGRESS HAS CATALOGED THE G. P. PUTNAM'S SONS EDITON AS FOLLOWS:
Birney, Betty G.
Spring according to Humphrey / Betty G. Birney
pages cm
ISBN 9780399257988 (hardcover)
Summary: "To Humphrey and the students at Longfellow School, spring seems impossibly
late this year. Fortunately, planning a school Family Fun Night keeps the students (and
classroom pets) busy as they look for signs of the changing seasons"—Provided by
publisher.
[1. Spring—Fiction. 2. Hamsters—Fiction. 3. Schools—Fiction.]
I. Title.
PZ7. B5229Sp 2016
[Fic]—dc23
2015009118

Puffin Books ISBN 9780147517777

Printed in the United States of America

5 7 9 10 8 6

Design by Annie Ericsson

THANKS-THANKS-THANKS
to my editor, Susan Kochan,
for a dozen Humphrey books and counting!

Contents

March Misery

I didn't hear Mrs. Brisbane's key turn as she opened the door that morning. I was sound asleep, snuggled under the bedding in my cage. It had been COLD-COLD-COLD all night and I was dreaming of summer. Nice, warm, sunny summer.

Suddenly, I heard Mrs. Brisbane say, "Be-Careful-Kelsey. Your boots are wet."

And then she said, "Simon! Slow down. I don't want anyone sliding across the floor and getting hurt."

I poked my head out of the bedding and saw Mrs. Brisbane and most of my fellow classmates in Room 26 coming through the door. They wore caps and gloves, heavy jackets and boots.

"Sorry I was late," Mrs. Brisbane continued. "The ice had traffic backed up. I'm glad you all made it here safely."

Ice? Just the word gave me a chill.

My cage sits near the windowsill, so I decided to peek outside.

"Eeek!" I squeaked.

"BOING!" my neighbor Og chimed in.

For most of the year, I look out at trees and grass and the school parking lot. In the fall, the trees are red and gold. In the winter, they have branches that are either bare or tipped with snow.

But on this March day, the trees were silvery icicles, sparkling like diamonds. The brown earth glistened with a thin coating of shiny crystals.

"I *hate* winter!" Daniel said.

I turned and saw my friends all seated at their tables.

"I like deep snow, when you can make snowmen and go sledding," Helpful-Holly said.

"I only like snow when we get a snow day," Do-It-Now-Daniel said.

A lot of my friends agreed.

"I think ice is cool," Simon said. "I skated down our driveway this morning without any skates!"

"Oooh, that's dangerous," Calm-Down-Cassie said. "My mom slipped on the ice and broke her arm a couple of years ago."

Mrs. Brisbane nodded. "It *is* dangerous, Simon."

Simon just shrugged and said, "I think it's fun."

"I like snow." Not-Now-Nicole shivered. "But I don't like ice. It's so . . . *icy.*"

The way she said it made me shiver, too.

Mrs. Brisbane walked over to the windowsill and peered down at my cage. "Are you warm enough,

Humphrey?" she asked. "It might be too cold for you next to the window."

"I'm all right," I answered. "As long as I have nice, warm bedding and my fur coat."

Unfortunately, since I am the classroom hamster, all she heard was "SQUEAK-SQUEAK-SQUEAK!"

Then Mrs. Brisbane turned to Og. He's the pet frog in Room 26. "How are you, Og? I know frogs don't like cold weather."

Og hopped up and down and made his usual weird sound. "BOING-BOING!"

Mrs. Brisbane turned back to the class. "Well, I don't like snow or ice when it makes me late for school."

Tell-the-Truth-Thomas waved his hand and our teacher called on him.

"It's the beginning of March! It's not supposed to snow in March," he complained.

Mrs. Brisbane smiled. "But sometimes it *does* snow. Have you heard the saying 'March comes in like a lion but goes out like a lamb'?"

"What?" I squeaked.

Some of the students sitting close to me giggled.

"It means that at the beginning of March, we often have some wild weather roaring in. But by the time April rolls around, the weather is usually mild, like a lamb," she explained.

Mrs. Brisbane is unsqueakably smart! How does she know so much?

Small-Paul Fletcher raised his hand. "Meteorologists say that extreme winter weather is usually over around the end of February here," he said. "But it has been known to snow in March. Besides, this was a mix of freezing rain and snow."

Small-Paul is SMART-SMART-SMART. Maybe he'll be a meteorologist someday. But wait—don't they study meteors from outer space?

Mrs. Brisbane nodded. "Meteorologists study weather," she said. "So they would know."

Rolling-Rosie raised her hand. "I don't like ice. It's hard to stop my wheelchair sometimes."

I was surprised, because Rolling-Rosie is great at handling her wheelchair. She even knows how to pop a wheelie!

"Does anybody know when the first day of spring is?" Mrs. Brisbane asked.

I glanced out the window again. "It's definitely not today!" I squeaked.

"Too far away!" Just-Joey grumbled.

Again Small-Paul raised his hand. "March twentieth," he said.

Some of my friends groaned.

"That's weeks away!" Stop-Talking-Sophie said.

I was still feeling cold and shivery, so I jumped on my wheel and began to spin. That always gets my whiskers wiggling again.

The door opened and Hurry-Up-Harry Ito walked in.

"Sorry I'm late," he said. "We were stuck in lots of traffic." He handed Mrs. Brisbane a piece of paper. "I have a note from the office."

Mrs. Brisbane nodded. "Go take off your wet jacket and boots," she said.

Harry strolled to the cloakroom. I think he could have hurried up a little more, but that's just the way he is.

"Maybe spring will come faster if we pay attention to the signs that the season is beginning," Mrs. Brisbane said. "And I also want to tell you about something to look forward to."

There were murmurings around the room. I could tell she'd gotten my classmates' interest. Mrs. Brisbane always does!

"Tell us—please!" Kelsey said.

"We need good news," Felipe added.

"PLEASE-PLEASE-PLEASE!" I begged her.

Mrs. Brisbane smiled. "Longfellow School is having a Family Fun Night in April. There will be games, prizes, and pizza, and your whole family is invited."

"I like pizza!" Thomas said. "As long as it doesn't have mushrooms." He made a face and everybody laughed.

"There will be lots more to do than eat pizza," Mrs. Brisbane continued. "And each classroom has to come up with an activity or game. It will take some work, but it will also be fun."

The news seemed to please my friends. I don't know

much about Family Fun Nights or pizza or mushrooms, but I do know about having fun. I like it!

Tall-Paul raised his hand. "What night of the week is it?" he asked.

"It's a Thursday," our teacher answered.

Tall-Paul moaned. "I figured."

"What's wrong?" Mrs. Brisbane asked.

"My mom's a nurse and she works Thursday nights. She could come on Wednesday, though," he replied.

"I don't think we can change the date at this point," Mrs. Brisbane said. "Maybe she can switch with somebody."

Paul shook his head. "It's hard to change days. She's going to be disappointed."

I think everybody in Room 26 was disappointed for Paul G. I certainly was!

"Well, my dad probably can't come. I only see him on weekends," Just-Joey said.

"I know it's hard when not everyone can make it, but I promise you'll still have fun," Mrs. Brisbane said.

"Yeah," Thomas agreed. "You can still eat pizza! Unless it has mushrooms."

Then Mrs. Brisbane went back to talking about spring and assigned all of us in her class to start looking for signs of the season and writing our observations.

"Don't forget to use all of your senses," she said. "Sight, smell, taste, feel, touch. When you find a sign of spring, write down the date and what you observed. Then either attach a photo or make a drawing of it. I'll be posting them on the bulletin board."

Slow-Down-Simon waved his hand and Mrs. Brisbane called on him.

"You can't take a picture of a smell," he said.

Mrs. Brisbane agreed. "Then use your words to describe it. But if you can get a picture of the thing that smelled, that would be great."

"Simon's feet!" someone said. I'm not sure, but I think it was Tall-Paul. I think he meant it as a joke, because everybody giggled, including Simon.

"BOING-BOING!" Og said in his twangy voice. I guess he got the joke, too.

Then Mrs. Brisbane moved on to talking about math and carrying numbers. I was way too sleepy to carry anything, so I crawled into my little sleeping hut for a morning nap.

While I dozed, I had a dream. All my friends from Room 26 were coming up to my cage and introducing me to their family members. Of course, because I spend each weekend at a different student's house, I knew most of them.

"Humphrey, here's my mom," they said. Or "Humphrey, this is my dad."

I met everybody in my dream from brothers and sisters to aunts and uncles and grandparents of all shapes and sizes. Humans have so many relatives, I don't know how they keep them all straight! And each family is different in a special way.

When I woke up, I had a funny feeling. Where were my mom and dad, my sisters and brothers? Did I have aunts and uncles and cousins?

As far as I could tell, all I had were my human friends and Og the Frog. I consider him a good friend, but I'm pretty sure we're not related. We certainly don't look alike.

I have beautiful golden fur. He is green and has no fur at all. How does he stay warm?

I have a tiny mouth and tiny eyes. Og's eyes are HUGE and so is his mouth.

I say, "SQUEAK."

He says, "BOING!"

No, we're definitely not related.

~⁓~

During recess, my friends didn't go out to the playground as usual. They stayed inside and played FUN-FUN-FUN board games and card games.

While they were playing, I glanced out the window again and was amazed to see the sun shining brightly. The tree branches dripped as the ice melted.

Maybe spring was on the way after all.

I crossed my toes and hoped.

~⁓~

By the time Aldo arrived that night to clean Room 26, all of the ice had melted. (There are streetlamps that help me see the street and parking lot.)

"*Mamma mia,*" he said. "What a day! I was late to class because of all the ice. And I can't afford to be late to class. After all, I'm about to graduate from college!"

Aldo always does an amazing job of keeping Room 26 clean. Of course, since he was going to college so he could become a teacher like Mrs. Brisbane, he wouldn't be cleaning classrooms once he graduated.

"It won't be long now, Humphrey, and I'll be the father of twins!" he said.

I was happy that Aldo was having twins and going to college, but I wasn't so happy for me. After all, Aldo brought Og and me treats every night. That night, he brought little zucchini sticks—crunchy and sweet! Og got some Froggy Fish Sticks. He loves them—which is another reason I know we're not related. Ick!

Aldo sat down and unwrapped his sandwich. "I wonder if my twins will ever realize how hard I've worked to get ahead."

"Of course they will," I squeaked. "They'll be proud!"

"I'm already applying for teaching jobs in the fall," Aldo said. "But I have to say, every time I think about leaving Longfellow School, I think of how much I'll miss you two."

My heart did a little flip-flop. "I'll miss you, too," I squeaked.

"BOING-BOING-BOING!" Og agreed.

Aldo finished his sandwich in silence. And when he was gone, I felt a teeny-tiny bit sad. I didn't care that much about the treats, but I would MISS-MISS-MISS seeing Aldo—and his amazing mustache!

HUMPHREY'S SPRING THINGS
I'm REALLY-REALLY-REALLY happy that soon there will be spring.
But I don't know what to think about this family thing!

The Waiting Game

~~~~~~

After Aldo's car had left the parking lot, I decided to go see Gigi. She's the guinea pig in Ms. Mac's first-grade class.

"Og, I'm going to check on Gigi," I said. "But I won't be gone long because she has to get to sleep."

I'm HAPPY-HAPPY-HAPPY that hamsters don't sleep all through the night, because that's the time I have my biggest adventures! I'm only sorry that Og worries about me when I'm gone.

I jiggled my lock-that-doesn't-lock and scurried across the table. I took a deep breath and slid down the table leg to the floor.

I scrambled across the room and crawled under the door, then raced down the darkened hallway to Room 12. Once I was inside, I hurried to the table by the window.

I wasn't sure if Gigi was awake or not, so I quietly squeaked, "Gigi? Hi, it's me, Humphrey."

"Hi, Humphrey," she replied in her soft voice. I'm pawsitively thrilled that I can understand Gigi. I can understand humans, but they can't understand me the way Gigi does. And I *still* haven't figured out frog language.

"I was hoping you'd visit," she said. "Can you come up here?"

Getting up to the tabletop is always dangerous, but I grabbed onto the blinds cord, which hung almost on the floor, and slowly swung higher and higher until I could let go and leap onto the table near Gigi.

"Did you see the ice this morning?" I asked. "Here it is March and we had an ice storm! All my friends in Room Twenty-six can't wait for spring to come."

"What's spring?" Gigi asked.

She's a little younger than I am and hasn't been in school very long.

"It's what comes after winter," I explained. "It gets warmer and greener and things start to grow again."

"Oh," Gigi said. "I don't know about those things."

"You will," I assured her. "Just pay attention in class. Ms. Mac is a great teacher."

"I know," Gigi said. "I love Ms. Mac."

I love Ms. Mac, too, even though she broke my heart once and moved away. Luckily, she came back. She's not my teacher anymore, but she still visits me sometimes.

Gigi suddenly yawned.

"Sorry, Humphrey," she said. "You know I go to bed early."

"I know," I replied. "And I like to stay up late."

"It's not easy to sleep with the blinds open," she said. "The streetlight shines in my cage and wakes me up."

Mrs. Brisbane used to close the blinds at night, but Aldo started opening them so I could see outside. I guess Aldo opens them for Gigi, too.

"Maybe I can close them," I said.

I examined the blinds. Up until that moment, I'd only used the cord as a way to make my way up to the tables in Room 26 and Room 12. I usually gently swing myself up to table level. I don't weigh very much and I've never had a problem.

But in order to make the blinds come down, I gave the cord a hard yank. Nothing happened, so I pulled it to the left. Suddenly the blinds crashed down and the cord lifted me up off the table. I was hanging in midair!

"Humphrey! What are you doing up there?" Gigi asked.

"I'm stuck," I said. I was feeling SCARED-SCARED-SCARED.

If I let go, I'd fall down on the table and I might hurt myself.

If I pulled harder, the cord might lift me up even higher!

I knew I couldn't hang on forever. I needed a Plan and I needed it quickly!

I looked around to see if there was something soft on the table. There were stacks of papers and a few books, as well as Gigi's guinea pig food.

Then I saw it: a box of nice, soft-looking tissues. Unfortunately, they were too far away for me to jump on.

"Gigi, have you ever tried jiggling your lock open?" I asked.

"No," she said. "Why?"

"If you have a lock-that-doesn't-lock, like mine, then you could help me," I said.

"Oh, I want to help! What should I do?" Gigi asked.

I told her to push up, push down and JIGGLE-JIGGLE-JIGGLE the lock. Nothing happened.

"Try leaning against the door with all your weight," I suggested. "Then jiggle the door."

Gigi put her body against the door and then she wiggled and jiggled and—oh, my! The door swung wide open!

Gigi gasped. "Now what?"

I asked her to push the tissue box until it was directly under me.

She didn't waste any time. She slid the box toward me until it was right under my legs.

"That's it," I said.

I closed my eyes and let go, dropping down onto a very soft bed of tissues.

"Are you okay?" Gigi asked.

I sneezed because a little tissue fluff got in my nose.

"I'm fine," I said. "Thanks for saving me." I climbed out of the box and hopped onto the table.

"I was scared," Gigi whispered. "But you're very brave."

"I was a little bit scared, too," I said. "Thanks for helping me. I promise I'll never make that mistake again!"

Then I realized that we had another problem. The top tissue where I landed wouldn't be clean. (Even though I'm a very clean hamster.) I wouldn't want one of my human friends to use it.

Luckily, I had another Plan. Gigi and I pushed the tissue box on its side and I gently removed the top one.

"Won't Ms. Mac notice that the box is on its side?" Gigi asked.

"Yes, but she won't know that we did it," I explained.

I was going to push the used tissue onto the floor, but I didn't want Aldo to get in trouble. I pushed it under the bag of food instead.

"So now that you're out of your cage, would you like to go on an adventure?" I asked. "We can just slide down the table leg."

Gigi looked horrified. "Guinea pigs don't slide or climb. It's too scary."

That seemed strange, because hamsters like me LOVE-LOVE-LOVE adventures.

My friend yawned. "Sorry, Humphrey, but it's my bedtime. Nighty-night."

She crawled into her cage and I pushed the door shut.

Yep, the lock looked locked, just like mine.

When I got back to Room 26, Og greeted me with a series of BOINGs. I was used to the strange sound he makes, but he was unusually loud.

"Sorry I was gone so long. I was just, um, hanging around," I said. I tried to make a joke, but dangling in midair hadn't been funny at all.

I'd never look at a blinds cord the same way again!

Later, I got out my little notebook to write about my fur-raising experience. I loved writing by the warm glow of the streetlight. Hamsters and guinea pigs may understand one another, but we're different in so many ways.

⁓

My classmates and I spent a lot of time looking for signs of spring, but we didn't come up with much.

"My mom ordered seeds for her garden," Felipe said one day. "But she can't plant them yet."

"I'd still say that was a sign of spring," Mrs. Brisbane said.

March was a funny month. We'd have sunshine and warmer weather for a few days. Then suddenly, it would rain and turn cold and gloomy.

"Og, have you seen one single sign of spring yet?" I asked after two weeks of feeling frustrated.

He replied with a very bored-sounding "BOING."

"Me either," I said.

My friends were as frustrated as I was.

"You'd think the leaves would be budding," Holly complained.

Not-Now-Nicole sighed. "You'd think the flowers would be blooming."

"Where are the robins?" Rosie wondered.

Mrs. Brisbane smiled. "They'll be here soon. The first day of spring is coming up."

Small-Paul raised his hand. "I was reading up on the average temperatures for March here, and this is completely normal."

There were several loud groans.

"It's not my fault," Paul said. "It's a scientific fact."

"We don't blame you, Paul," Rolling-Rosie said. "But why does science have to be so . . . *scientific*?"

At least she made everybody laugh.

A few days before the first day of spring, it snowed . . . again.

"This is not fair!" Harry groaned.

Daniel agreed. "At least it could have snowed enough for them to call off school!"

Mrs. Brisbane went on to talk about math problems and I gazed out at the snow. It wasn't very deep and there were patches of brown showing through.

White and brown. Brown and white. White and . . . *purple*?

"Look!" I squeaked. "LOOK-LOOK-LOOK!"

I knew that the purple thing could be a wrapper from somebody's lunch. Or anything someone might have dropped. I climbed to the tippy top of my cage for a better look.

"Humphrey seems excited," Mrs. Brisbane said, hurrying to the table. "Is something wrong?"

"NO-NO-NO!" I squeaked. "It's a sign!"

She didn't understand me, of course, but Og joined in with a "BOING-BOING!"

"They're looking outside," our teacher said. "But what are they looking at?"

The students rushed to the window to look.

Og and I continued to make a lot of noise.

"It's purple! It's spring!" I squeaked.

"BOING-BOING-BOING!" Og added.

Rosie leaned forward in her wheelchair and pressed her nose against the window. "Look!" She pointed. "It's a purple flower coming through the snow!"

The classroom buzzed with excitement.

"Where?" Thomas asked.

"Yeah, where?" Sophie said.

"I see it." Mrs. Brisbane pointed, too. "Over there, near the base of the tall tree."

I heard lots of *ooh*s and *aah*s.

"I think we should go out and see for ourselves," Mrs. Brisbane said.

"Yes, we should!" I squeaked.

It seemed to take them forever to put on coats and hats, boots and gloves, and then tramp outside to see the flower.

My friends were excited and so was I—until I realized that Og and I weren't going outside with them.

The cold isn't good for either one of us. I knew that, but I couldn't help but wish that I could put on a coat and hat and boots and gloves and join them!

Og and I silently stared out the window until we saw Mrs. Brisbane lead my friends to the little spot of purple.

Everyone crouched down to stare at the purple bloom. Mrs. Brisbane snapped a photo.

And then she did something wonderful. She looked right up at our window and waved.

I don't think she could see me, but I waved back.

"BOING!" Og twanged. "BOING-BOING!"

I LOVE-LOVE-LOVE Mrs. Brisbane. And at that moment, I knew that she LOVED-LOVED-LOVED me.

And Og, too, of course.

When my friends returned to Room 26, their cheeks were rosy and their eyes sparkled with excitement.

"What did you call that flower, Mrs. Brisbane?" Tell-the-Truth-Thomas asked.

"I believe it was a crocus," she said. "Let's look it up."

Once the gloves and hats and boots and scarves were off, Mrs. Brisbane opened a big book and turned page after page.

"Here," she said. "What do you think?"

My friends all leaned in around her desk, where she had opened the book.

"I wish I could see it," I told Og.

"BOING-BOING!" he replied.

"It's definitely a crocus," Helpful-Holly said. "And to think, it poked its little head up through the snow."

The door to Room 26 swung open and in walked the Most Important Person at Longfellow School, our principal, Mr. Morales!

"I saw you all tramping through the snow," he said. "I wondered what you were looking at."

He was smiling, so I knew he wasn't upset.

"There's a purple crocus in the snow!" Stop-Talking-Sophie said. "It's the first sign of spring—and it was beautiful! I'll show you!"

She led Mr. Morales to the window and pointed. "It's that little bit of purple near the tree."

Mrs. Brisbane was behind us. "Humphrey and Og seemed to spot it first," she said.

"Because they are very wise and observant," Mr. Morales said.

"Thank you," I squeaked.

"BOING!" Og said.

Then I heard voices chanting, "It's spring! It's spring! It's such a wonderful thing!"

I looked over and saw Rosie, Holly, Nicole and Kelsey joining hands and repeating, "It's spring! It's spring! It's such wonderful thing!"

Mr. Morales smiled and said, "I agree. I sit in my office and work at my desk and talk on my phone, and sometimes, I never even look out the window. Thank you for showing me a wonderful thing."

It's funny how a little purple flower in the snow can make people so happy. Hamsters and frogs, too!

After Mr. Morales left, my classmates started writing about the first sign of spring.

Mrs. Brisbane wrote *crocus* on the chalkboard. She also passed around purple crayons for my friends to share.

They were VERY-VERY-VERY quiet until they left for lunch.

While they were gone, I took out my notebook.

I didn't have a purple crayon, but I think I did a pretty good job of drawing a crocus without one!

HUMPHREY'S SPRING THINGS

It almost took forever to see a sign of spring,
But now that it has happened, it's such a thrilling thing!

The Humster

At the end of the day, Mrs. Brisbane handed out flyers to all my friends. "This is the information about Family Fun Night. Please share it with your family so they can mark the date on their calendars."

As soon as the papers were in my friends' backpacks, the bell rang and they raced out of the room.

Slow-Down-Simon was the first student out, as usual.

Hurry-Up-Harry was the last student to gather up his coat and hat and leave Room 26.

Mrs. Brisbane straightened the papers on her desk. Then she came over to the window and looked out. "I hope we see more signs of spring soon," she said. "We usually do by now."

"We saw the crocus!" I reminded her.

Mrs. Brisbane looked at me and smiled. "I imagine that you're ready for spring, too." She looked over at Og. "How about you, Og?"

Og didn't answer. He just dived into the water side of his tank and started swimming.

Mrs. Brisbane chuckled. "At least you have a swimming pool year-round."

Hamsters like me don't like swimming, but I guess humans and frogs do.

After Mrs. Brisbane was gone for the day—and before Aldo came in to clean—I told Og I was going to visit Gigi. I wanted to make sure she saw the flower in the snow before it was dark.

"Hi, Humphrey!" Gigi happily squeaked as I slid under the door.

I scurried over to the table and swung myself up.

I was a little out of breath when I said, "Did you see the first sign of spring?"

"No," Gigi said, looking around her cage. "Where is it?"

"Outside," I replied.

Luckily, the blinds were open. Gigi looked toward the window and twisted her head from side to side. "I don't see anything but a little snow on the ground."

"Open your door," I said. "Remember how?"

Gigi leaned against the door, wiggling and jiggling until it popped open.

"I can't believe that really works," she said.

The two of us moved close to the window and looked out.

"Look over to the right, near that tall tree. There's something purple on the ground," I explained.

Gigi squinted and stared, and then she said, "What is that?"

I explained about the crocus being the first flower of spring, pushing through the snow.

"I didn't think flowers grew when it was cold," Gigi said.

I explained that they usually don't, but sometimes they pop up right through the snow.

"It's beautiful," Gigi whispered.

We sat for a while, staring out at the little speck of purple in the white snow.

Finally, I asked, "Did Ms. Mac tell the class about Family Fun Night?"

"Uh-huh," Gigi said. "It sounds like fun, but will there be a lot of people there? And will it be noisy?"

"Yes." I laughed. "I think there will be a lot of people, and when people are having fun, they're usually noisy."

Gigi giggled. "That's true."

She paused for a while, and then she said, "Families are awfully nice."

I nodded. "I've been to homes with lots of wonderful families. I always get a warm feeling in my toes when I see families together."

"Me too," Gigi agreed. "Of course, I don't have a family."

"I don't have one, either," I said. "But I must have had a family sometime. I mean, as mammals, we had a mother and a father and probably brothers and sisters."

"I can't remember." Gigi sounded sad.

"Neither can I," I said. "But everybody has a family somewhere."

Gigi went back into her cage. I helped her shut the door so it looked as if it hadn't been opened.

"I'm sorry the blinds are open," I said.

"At least I saw the crocus," she said. "And Ms. Mac said she left a note for Aldo to close the blinds when he's done cleaning. She knows I need my sleep."

Leave it to Ms. Mac to understand a classroom pet.

"Sleep well," I told her.

When I got back to my cage in Room 26, I told Og all about my visit.

"BOING-BOING-BOING!" he twanged when I talked about families.

"Do you remember your family?" I asked him.

He didn't answer. He just dived into the water with a huge splash.

"I'm sure you had a nice one," I said as I returned to my cage. "I'm sure we all did, if we could only remember."

~·~·~

When Aldo cleaned the classroom that night, he was restless. As he swept the floor, he muttered to himself, but, of course, Og and I could hear him.

"It's all happening at once," he said. "Final exams, graduation, job hunting and two new babies! It's too much."

My whiskers wiggled as I heard him talking. Didn't Aldo want to graduate from college, get a better job and be the father of twins?

Aldo emptied the floor sweepings into the trash can. "What if I fail?" he said.

"You won't!" I squeaked. "NEVER-NEVER-NEVER!"

Og chimed in with a very loud "BOING-BOING!"

I was surprised when Aldo laughed.

"You two," he said. "You never let a friend down, do you?"

"I certainly hope not!" I squeaked back.

Even though Aldo couldn't understand me, I was warmly rewarded with a sweet and tender piece of lettuce from the sandwich he ate on his break.

"Thanks, pals," he told us as he threw a Froggy Fish Stick into my friend's tank.

"You're welcome, Aldo," I replied.

◦~◦~◦

On Friday afternoon, I saw the biggest grin I've ever seen!

It was Joey smiling when Mrs. Brisbane announced that I'd be going home with him for the weekend.

I was delighted to see him so happy, but I was also a little worried. Sometimes he talked about his dog, Skipper, who was very good at catching a Frisbee with his teeth. Skipper must have large and sharp teeth to catch something flying through the air at great speed.

I'm not fond of dogs with large, sharp teeth because I've had bad experiences with them in the past.

"I never thought it would happen," Joey said as he picked up my cage. "I wish we could go home right away, but I have to go to the after-school program. You can come with me."

I'd never heard of an after-school program before, but anything that has to do with school is FUN-FUN-FUN to me.

Joey carefully carried my cage (and his coat) down the hall.

26

The gym is an enormous room with bleachers and a stage. It wasn't my first time there, but it was my first time there for the after-school program.

I was happy to see many of my friends. Calm-Down-Cassie, Tell-the-Truth-Thomas, Hurry-Up-Harry and Helpful-Holly from my class were there. But so were some friends from last year's class: Raise-Your-Hand-Heidi, Don't-Complain-Mandy, Pay-Attention-Art, Speak-Up-Sayeh and Sit-Still-Seth.

They all seemed so happy to see me. As soon as Joey put my cage down on a table, everyone gathered around.

"Humphrey the Hamster," Art said.

"It's Humphrey Dumpty," Mandy said. That was the nickname A.J. had given me.

"No, he's the *Hum*ster," Harry said. That was a new nickname I'd never heard before.

"The Humster! The Humster!" my friends began to chant.

I liked my silly new nickname.

Their chanting stopped suddenly when a loud whistle blasted and my small hamster ears began to vibrate.

"Ow!" I squeaked.

Of course, I knew who blew that whistle. I'd seen it—and heard it—many times before.

Mrs. Wright, the PE teacher and owner of the whistle, leaned over my cage. "What is the hamster doing in my gym?"

I hopped on my wheel and squeaked, "Getting some exercise!"

I braced myself in case she blew the whistle, but instead, she leaned in closer.

"Well, at least it's getting some exercise." Then she stood up and looked around. "Who brought this animal to the gym?"

Joey stepped forward. "I did. I'm taking him home for the weekend, but my mom won't be here until five-thirty. So I thought he should come with me."

Mrs. Wright shook her head. "I wish Mrs. Brisbane would clear these things with me. Couldn't he have stayed in the classroom?"

"Yes," Joey answered. "But Mrs. Brisbane locks the door when she leaves, so how would I get him out?"

"Yes, how?" I squeaked at Mrs. Wright, even though, to squeak the truth, I'm a bit afraid of her.

"*No pets* allowed in the after-school program," she said. "Can you imagine what this gym would be like with dogs and cats and rabbits and hamsters running loose around the gym?"

When she put it that way, I could see her point. I didn't want to be running around with dogs and cats in the gym or anywhere else!

Joey looked down at my cage. "What should I do?"

Mrs. Wright sighed. "Well, he's here now, so I guess this time he'll have to stay. But never again."

Sometimes Mrs. Wright's voice made me shiver and quiver, because I'd worry that she'd blow that loud whistle.

"I have an idea," Joey said to Mrs. Wright.

She had her hand on the whistle as she looked down at him.

"We could build a hamster maze for Humphrey," he said. "He loves that."

"A hamster maze?" she asked in a way that made me think she didn't approve of hamsters *or* mazes.

"We put up books or bricks or whatever to make the maze and watch Humphrey run through it. Maybe we could make a human maze, too," Joey said.

Mrs. Wright thought for a moment. "I guess that would keep us all active and out of trouble," she said.

Keeping active was REALLY-REALLY-REALLY important to her. That's one thing we have in common!

Before I knew it, there was a lovely maze on the gymnasium floor, made of gymnastics mats and backpacks and cones and I don't know what!

There I was, running through it as fast as my paws would take me.

And there were my friends, all cheering me on.

It wasn't until I got to the end that Mrs. Wright blew her whistle.

Eeek, that was loud! But when my friends shouted, "Yay, Humster! Yay, Humster!" I felt hamster-iffic!

Next, my friends all ran through the maze, and I think Mrs. Wright was pretty happy to see them moving.

"Faster, Harry! You can do it! Go for it, Mandy!" she shouted.

When she wasn't blowing her whistle, she actually seemed like a very nice human.

The time passed quickly, so when Just-Joey's mom showed up, I couldn't believe it. It was five-thirty and time to go home.

"Wait until you meet Skipper." Joey put a warm blanket over my cage as we headed to the car.

Meet a dog? With sharp teeth? I *could* wait!

HUMPHREY'S SPRING THINGS
It's fun to be with friends and run a maze,
But when it comes to dogs, I'd like to wait a few more days!

The BIG-BIG-BIG Oops

This will be a fun weekend, Humphrey," Just-Joey told me as he carried my cage to the car. "Right, Mom?"

I couldn't hear very well because of the blanket, but I'm pretty sure she said, "Yes!"

We drove for a while and then the car stopped.

"I've waited for this a long time," Joey said.

"I know," his mom answered. "It was just hard to find the right weekend. It's a long way to your dad's house. I don't think Humphrey would be comfortable on such a long drive. But your dad had to work on a special project, so you're with me this weekend for a change."

Joey picked up the cage and I could feel him carry me up the sidewalk. I heard his mother put the key in the door. My whiskers wiggled and my tail twitched as I braced myself for Skipper's barks. Dog barks can be as painful to my ears as a whistle blast.

But there was no barking. Where was Skipper?

Once we were in the house, Joey uncovered my

cage. "This is my house, Humphrey," he said. "It's just an ordinary house, I guess. Nothing special."

"It's great!" I said. My eyes darted around the room, searching for a glimpse of Skipper.

Joey's mom leaned down to look at me. "Hello, Humphrey," she said. "You're just as handsome as Joey said you are."

I knew right away that I LIKED-LIKED-LIKED her.

"Show Mom how you can spin," Joey told me.

I leaped onto my wheel and started running.

"Wow, look at him go," Joey's mom said. "That's better than an hour at the gym."

Joey looked around. "Where's Skipper?"

"Yes, where's Skipper?" I squeaked.

"Oh, Becca offered to take him for a walk," his mom said. "Wasn't that nice?"

"Yes!" I squeaked.

I know how much my classmates love their pet cats and dogs. But much of the time, they aren't hamster friendly. In fact, they are usually hamster scary! So whoever Becca was, I silently thanked her. I crossed my toes and hoped it would be a very long walk.

Joey leaned down close to my cage. "Becca lives across the street," he said. "She'll be back soon with Skipper. I can't wait for you to meet him."

"Eeek!" I didn't mean to squeak, but I couldn't help it.

"I have so much to show you," Joey told me. "I want you to see my room, and Skipper catching a Frisbee."

"Could we skip the Frisbee part?" I asked.

Unfortunately, all that Joey heard was SQUEAK-SQUEAK-SQUEAK.

He carried my cage to his room and gave me a tour.

"Here's my bed, Humphrey," he said. "And my desk. And my dresser. Oh, and here's my closet."

I appreciated the tour, but when humans carry my cage, it swings back and forth and my tummy feels a little strange. I was happy when Joey set my cage on his desk and I wasn't swaying so much.

"Is everything okay?" Joey's mom asked from the hallway.

"Yep," Just-Joey said.

"Yep," I squeaked. "So far!"

I hopped on my wheel for another good spin—which helps me relax.

"I sure would like to have a hamster like you for a pet," Joey said, settling on the bed.

I thought it would be very nice to be Joey's pet, but he already had a pet dog.

And I LOVE-LOVE-LOVE my job as a classroom pet!

I heard a pitter-pitter-patter and, before I knew it, a furry creature raced through the bedroom door.

"Hi, Skipper," Joey said. "Meet Humphrey."

I braced myself as he trotted toward my cage.

Skipper was a medium-sized dog, white with brown spots.

He looked up at the cage and wagged his tail.

He raised his nose and sniffed, so I scurried to the back of my cage to get as far away from him as I could. You can't be too careful.

All the while, Joey talked to Skipper, explaining that I'm a hamster and I live in his classroom.

Skipper wagged some more and then he did something unexpected. He trotted out of the room!

I've met a few dogs nose to nose in the past, and they were *all* interested in me. In fact, they wouldn't leave me alone. They had bad breath and big teeth, and they all looked as if they thought I'd make a tasty little snack.

I realized for the first time that, like humans and hamsters, dogs are not all alike.

Maybe this would be a fun weekend after all!

~•~•~

The next morning, when Joey woke up, his mom came into the room and asked him what he wanted to do for the day. Skipper was nowhere in sight.

"I really want to take Humphrey to the backyard to watch Skipper catch a Frisbee," Joey said.

His mom shook her head. "That would be fun, but it's too cold for Humphrey to go outside."

That was unsqueakably nice of her because I didn't want my whiskers to freeze over!

"How about your homework?" she asked.

"Signs of spring!" I squeaked.

Joey's mom laughed. "Humphrey seems to know your assignment."

34

"I do," I answered. "I write them in my notebook."

"We're supposed to be looking for signs of spring," Joey said. He stared out the window and sighed. "I sure haven't seen any yet—except for the flower we saw in the snow."

"A crocus!" I added, trying to be helpful.

"I don't think we'll find signs of spring in the house," she said. "Why don't we take Skipper out for a walk and see what we can find? We could go to the nature preserve over by Potter's Pond."

Joey glanced over at my cage. "What about Humphrey? I'm supposed to take care of him for the whole weekend."

"I think he'll be all right for an hour or two," his mom said. "Right, Humphrey?"

"RIGHT-RIGHT-RIGHT!" I answered. And I meant it, because I was feeling a little sleepy and was looking forward to a nice nap.

Before I knew it, they were gone and I was dozing in my sleeping hut.

✎

I'm not sure how long they were gone, but when Joey walked back into his room, I scrambled out of my sleeping hut.

"What did you find?" I asked.

Joey slumped down in a chair near my cage. "No signs of spring, except a couple of blades of grass," he said.

He looked discouraged, so I said, "That's a great beginning!"

I just wished he could understand me.

"I'll bet this is the latest spring in the history of the planet," he said. "And the planet is pretty old."

"Maybe," I squeaked.

Joey stared at me for a few seconds. "Humphrey, I really want you to see Skipper catch a Frisbee, but Mom won't let me take you outside. And she won't let me throw it inside."

It would have been nice to see the trick, but I didn't want to go outside in the cold. And I wasn't too sure about disks flying all over the room.

Suddenly, Joey sat up. "Hey! I could put your cage on the windowsill. I'll take Skipper outside this window and you can watch!"

It was such an unsqueakably great Plan, I wished I'd thought of it.

Soon my cage was right next to the window, about a foot above the bed.

It wasn't long before Joey raced out into the yard and waved his Frisbee at me. It was a flat, red circle with tooth marks around the edge.

Skipper was right behind Joey, looking like he was ready to play.

Joey looked at me, then raised the Frisbee and let it fly. It soared UP-UP-UP, and as it started to come DOWN-DOWN-DOWN, Skipper leaped WAY off the ground and caught it in his mouth.

"Bravo!" I squeaked, clapping my front paws together.

Joey looked toward the window and put his thumbs up. I knew that meant something good.

I could tell he was getting ready to throw the Frisbee again, but I was frustrated because the bars on my cage—which give me good protection—blocked my view a bit.

Quickly, I jiggled the lock-that-doesn't-lock and scrambled up the *outside* of my cage to the very top.

Ah! What a nice view.

Joey raised his arm and tossed the Frisbee. It went even higher this time, and as it started to come down, Skipper jumped WAY-WAY-WAY up in the air and caught it perfectly.

"Way to go!" I cheered, jumping up and down on top of my cage.

Uh-oh. The cage was wobbling.

I don't weigh much at all, but I guess all my jumping nudged the cage toward the edge of the windowsill.

All of a sudden, it started tipping over.

I flew off the cage and rolled a bit. I came to a stop close—but not too close—to the edge. I am unsqueak-ably lucky that beds are nice and soft.

My heart was pounding, but once I caught my breath, I looked over and saw a disaster!

My bedding and food were scattered across the bed-spread. Luckily, my water bottle hadn't leaked and my notebook was still firmly tucked behind the mirror.

OOPS!

I leaped to my feet and tried to push the cage upright, but it was no use.

I was in trouble. And so was Joey.

BIG-BIG-BIG trouble.

HUMPHREY'S SPRING THINGS

Eeek! This was an awful thing!

So far, I wasn't loving spring.

The Silly Specks

Joey's mom discovered the disaster first.

"Joey!" she yelled, tapping on the window. "Come in at once!"

"Hi!" I squeaked to let her know everything was all right.

"Poor Humphrey," she said, reaching her hand toward me. "I won't hurt you."

She didn't, either. She gently scooped me up in her hand, and Joey raced into the room.

"What's wrong?" he asked.

His mom wasn't happy. She pointed to the mess on the bed. "This," she said. "You put the cage on the windowsill and it fell off. Somehow, poor little Humphrey got out of his cage. And look at the mess!"

"I'm fine," I squeaked. "Really. It was exciting."

Joey looked surprised. "Mom, I made sure it was fine. Look, there's plenty of room for the cage to fit on the windowsill."

"You're going to clean this up now," she said. "Then I'll wash your bedspread."

"Sure," Joey said. "Don't be mad, Mom. I just wanted him to see Skipper catch the Frisbee."

Joey was true to his word. He's about the best cage cleaner in the world.

First, he made a little space for me on the table, surrounded by books so I couldn't scamper or fall off. Then he cleaned up the mess on the bed, washed my cage and put in new bedding.

Before long, my cage looked better than ever, and I was back home at last.

Joey's mom had to admit he'd done a great job. She was bundling up the bedspread when the doorbell rang. Skipper barked a little bit, but then he stopped. Good dog!

"I'll get it," she said.

"Me too," Joey said as he followed her out of the room.

I waited and waited and then Joey returned. His mom was right behind him, carrying a large aquarium.

"Humphrey, this is amazing!" Joey said as his mom set the aquarium next to my cage on the desk. "Wait till you see!"

"It is pretty amazing," Joey's mom agreed.

"I'd told my dad that we were looking for signs of spring, and he sent this kit with TWO tadpoles," Joey explained. "Tadpoles are found in ponds in the spring, and then they turn into frogs!"

Frogs? Like my friend Og?

I scrambled to the side of the cage to get a closer

look. All I saw was a little piece of jelly floating in the tank . . . with two black specks.

"They're just specks!" I said.

"See, Humphrey?" Joey said. "This is how Og started out."

"I don't think so," I squeaked back. There's no way a large green creature could start out as a tiny black speck.

"I know it's hard to believe, but we're going to see for ourselves," he said. "Wasn't it nice of my dad to send it to me?"

Joey's mom and dad were divorced and didn't live together anymore. In fact, Joey's dad lived in a whole different town.

"It was nice," his mom said. "But we'll have to read the instructions to make sure we know how to take care of these things."

Joey stared at the strange specks. I could tell by his eyes that he was unsqueakably excited.

Suddenly, he jumped up. "I have a great idea!" he cried. "I could take them to school and the whole class could watch the tadpoles turn into frogs."

"That's a great idea," his mom said. "Much better than keeping them here." I don't think Joey's mom was very excited about learning to take care of tadpoles. She quickly added, "I'll e-mail Mrs. Brisbane to see if it's all right with her."

Joey didn't even notice his mother leave the room. He was too busy staring at the specks.

Skipper raced through the door. I felt jumpy, but once again, he didn't even come close to the cage. He just flopped down on the floor and fell asleep. Whew!

Joey didn't take his eyes off the aquarium. "Humphrey, I can't wait to see those little specks grow heads and tails and feet and just keep growing until they are real frogs."

I crossed my paws and hoped they would, but I wasn't sure at all.

I had never seen Joey so excited! He's usually quiet, and sometimes I think he doesn't realize how many things he can do. He's good at art and knows a lot about animals and he's very good at taking care of me. In fact, I think he'd make a pawsitively great animal doctor!

Joey eagerly read the instruction booklet that came with the, um, thingies.

"Oh, I get it," he said as he read. Then he looked at me and said, "Here's how it works, Humphrey. These are like eggs in a yolk. They'll feed on the yolk and pretty soon they'll become tadpoles!"

"Eeek!" I squeaked.

Joey read on. "Any day now, they'll get legs and a head and, after a while, arms!"

"Frogs have arms?" I wondered.

"Then the tadpole will look like a small frog with a long tail," Joey said. "Wow, this is the most exciting thing that ever happened to me!"

It was nice to see Joey so HAPPY-HAPPY-HAPPY.

"Did I tell you they're leopard frogs?" Joey asked.

"NO-NO-NO!" I squeaked.

I have seen pictures of the creatures called *leopards*. They are strong and beautiful with spotted fur, but their teeth are large, sharp and fearsome. MUCH worse than the teeth of a dog. Just thinking about leopards made my tail twitch and my whiskers wiggle.

I may be friends with a frog, but I don't think I could ever be friends with a leopard.

"Does the book mention if leopard frogs have teeth?" I squeaked. How I wish Joey could understand me.

Og may have an enormous mouth, but at least he doesn't have teeth!

"It takes a while to turn into a frog, but it will sure be something to see," Joey said.

Then he leaped up. As he ran out of the room, he said, "I've got to call Dad to say thank you!"

I'm used to sitting in my cage next to a tank containing a frog.

I'm not used to sitting in my cage next to a tank containing specks.

I turned to stare at them, but they didn't say anything.

"Hello," I finally squeaked. "I'm Humphrey. I'm a hamster."

They didn't even say "BOING!" How rude.

∽✷∽

I wanted—I needed—to get a better look at the specks, but I waited until that night when Joey was in bed.

I hardly ever open my lock-that-doesn't-lock when a human is in the room, but I could see by the glow of Joey's night-light that he was sound asleep.

I jiggled my lock open without making any noise. Then I slowly walked over to the aquarium, which was lit by the night-light as well.

There they were: two specks in a clear jelly-like goo.

I stared at them, but they didn't move. They didn't do anything.

They looked like two eyeballs staring back.

They certainly looked more like eyeballs than frogs.

I watched for a while, but to squeak the truth, the specks were pretty boring, so I scurried back to my cage and quietly pulled the cage door shut.

It was hard to understand why Joey was so excited about the tadpoles.

But then, humans are *always* hard to understand.

◡◠◡

When Joey jumped up out of bed the next morning, he raced to the aquarium to look at the specks.

"Good morning, Joey," I squeaked.

"Hi, Humphrey," he said without even looking at me. "Just checking out the tadpoles."

He leaned in close and stared at them. I'm pretty sure they didn't do anything.

When he finally straightened up and looked at me, he said, "Nothing yet." Then he perked up. "Oh! I need to draw a picture of them for the bulletin board."

I didn't think it would take a long time to draw two specks. Seconds, maybe.

But Joey leaned over a piece of paper with his colored pencils and drew and drew and drew. He used several crayons, even though there wasn't much to draw.

At one point, Joey's mom said, "Hey, Joey—how about breakfast?"

"Coming soon," he called back. "I've got to get this right."

When he was finished, he inspected it and then nodded his head. "Not too bad." Then he jumped up and ran out of the room. "See you later, Humphrey!"

I was pretty sure that eating breakfast took a while, so once the coast was clear, I jiggled my lock-that-doesn't-lock and scurried over to look at Joey's drawing.

It's not easy for a small hamster to look at a large piece of paper, but I studied what Joey had drawn and it was . . . beautiful! Where I'd seen two specks in clear jelly, Joey had seen so much more!

The specks were black, but the jelly was yellow and light green and really beautiful.

When I glanced at the aquarium, I saw that the jelly really was yellow and green and shimmering.

I couldn't risk being caught outside of my cage, so I raced back and closed the door behind me.

When Joey returned from breakfast, he took some photos of the specks.

"I want to show Dad what they look like," he said.

Then he took a picture of me. I stood still and smiled. I'm not sure he could tell I was smiling, but Joey said, "Great!"

He raced out of the room again.

"I haven't seen him so excited in a long time," I squeaked out loud.

The specks had nothing to say.

HUMPHREY'S SPRING THINGS

Can a speck become a frog?
Did a speck turn into *Og*?

SWIM·SWIM·SWIM

On Monday, Joey's mom threw a small blanket over the aquarium and another one over my cage and I began my dark journey back to school.

"Mrs. Brisbane was excited about having the tadpoles," she said. "But I'm not sure we need the blankets. It's a beautiful day!"

"Really?" I squeaked. Because I couldn't see anything.

Once my cage was uncovered, I was back on the table by the windowsill in Room 26.

"BOING-BOING!" Og's strange voice rang out.

"Be prepared, Og!" I squeaked back at him. "You're going to see something surprising."

Joey's mom set the aquarium on the table between Og's tank and my cage, then hurried off to work.

Soon, all my classmates were crowded around the table, asking Joey what was in the aquarium.

Mrs. Brisbane told them to take their seats. "After the bell rings, we'll talk about our signs of spring. Then Joey will explain what's in the tank."

My friends looked disappointed as they went back to their tables.

I was pretty sure they'd be even more disappointed when they found out that there was nothing in the tank but two specks.

The bell rang and Mrs. Brisbane took attendance.

"Now can we see what's in the tank?" Slow-Down-Simon asked.

Mrs. Brisbane smiled and said, "Try to be a little bit patient. Now, raise your hand if you'd like to share a sign of spring that you found this weekend."

A lot of hands went up. Mrs. Brisbane called on Rolling-Rosie first.

"It's staying light longer in the evening. And it was so warm today, I didn't have to wear my winter coat—just a light jacket," she said.

"Yes." Mrs. Brisbane nodded. "The days start to get longer in the spring. Remember, we set our clocks forward an hour for daylight savings time. So the skies are light a lot longer now."

Hurry-Up-Harry raised his hand. "But it's darker in the morning. It's hard to get out of bed when it's dark." He yawned a big yawn.

Some of my friends laughed, but Mrs. Brisbane agreed. "I have to admit, it's hard for me to get up, too, Harry."

Lots of my classmates had seen leaves budding on trees, grass springing out of the ground and flowers growing.

Helpful-Holly said her mom had taken her shopping for spring clothes.

"That's a great sign of spring," Mrs. Brisbane said.

"The stores are full of Easter candy," Thomas said. "But my mom won't buy it for me. She says Easter is a long way off."

His comment brought more giggles.

Small-Paul got up and showed the class a new chart he'd made of spring temperatures over the last ten years. "We've been having average temperatures for spring," he said as he pointed to wavy lines and explained them.

At last, it was Joey's turn. "My dad sent me two signs of spring. May I show them now?" he asked Mrs. Brisbane.

Our teacher said yes, and Joey walked over to our table.

"In the spring, lots of animals come out of hibernation and have new babies," he said. "Including these!"

All eyes were on Joey as he pulled the small blanket off the aquarium.

I heard a gasp, then silence.

The only one who made a sound was Og. "BOING-BOING-BOING!"

"These are tadpoles," Joey said. "I mean, they're going to grow into tadpoles. And tadpoles grow into frogs. They just look like dots now, but pretty soon they'll grow tails and legs and start to become frogs."

Everybody was quiet until Og twanged, "BOING-BOING-BOING-BOING!"

That made everybody laugh.

Stop-Talking-Sophie's hand shot up. "Was Og a tadpole once?"

Joey nodded. "Sure. All frogs were."

My friends seemed surprised and so was I!

"Can we see them?" Felipe asked.

Mrs. Brisbane had my friends make a line so that each one could have a good look.

"You might be disappointed!" I squeaked. "They don't do much!"

One by one, they came up to the aquarium to look at the specks with Mrs. Brisbane and Joey.

"What's that goo?" Not-Now-Nicole asked.

"It's like the inside of an egg," Joey said. He looked up at Mrs. Brisbane. "Right?"

"Yes, I think so," she replied. "But we will all study tadpoles to learn more about them."

Suddenly, Og dived down in the water side of his tank and began splashing loudly.

"What's wrong with him?" Joey asked.

"Maybe he doesn't want any competition," Mrs. Brisbane said with a smile. "Or maybe he's excited to have new friends."

What's so exciting about two new friends when they're only specks? Having a hamster friend is much more interesting.

When Tall-Paul came up to the tank, he just shook his head. "It's hard to believe those two dots will become frogs like Og."

"BOING-BOING!" Og said.

"Right!" I agreed.

Joey explained that they wouldn't be exactly like

Og, because he was a green frog and they were leopard frogs.

"Wow!" Tall-Paul said. "Will they have spots?"

"Yep," Joey replied.

Helpful-Holly asked, "Will they be our classroom pets, like Humphrey and Og?"

"NO-NO-NO!" I squeaked. "They are nothing like Og and me!"

I'm sorry to admit it, but I didn't like the idea at all.

"They belong to Joey," Mrs. Brisbane said. "For now . . . let's just watch them grow."

I watched the specks that night, but I didn't see any changes.

"Nothing yet," I squeaked to my neighbor.

Og stayed strangely silent.

When Aldo came in to clean Room 26, he was surprised to find a new aquarium on the table between Og's tank and my cage.

"What is this?" he asked, peering at the specks.

"Two tadpoles!" I squeaked. Of course, I knew that he didn't understand me.

Aldo stared and stared and then he chuckled. "Tadpoles!" he said. "Twin tadpoles." He kept chuckling as he swept the floor. "Twins, twins everywhere. I think I'm seeing double!"

He turned in Og's direction. "How do you feel about twin frogs, Og?"

But Og just sat there like a rock.

Og was silent all night long.

The specks didn't change one bit. Were they really alive?

Although I'm usually active at night, Room 26 was so boring, I fell asleep. And I didn't wake up until sunlight was streaming through the window and Mrs. Brisbane opened the door.

"Morning!" she said in a cheery voice.

"Morning," I squeaked.

Og was still silent.

I glanced over and saw that Mrs. Brisbane carried a vase with some very colorful flowers in it. They were red, yellow, orange and purple.

"How are these for signs of spring?" she asked as she set the vase on her desk.

"Very nice!" I said.

By the time she took off her coat, Thomas and Felipe raced into the room.

"Look at this sign of spring." Thomas spread his arms wide and turned in a circle. "My mom didn't make me wear my winter jacket. I was getting really tired of that old thing. Besides, the arms were getting way too short! I won't be wearing that jacket anymore."

Mrs. Brisbane held up the vase of flowers. "Here's my sign of spring. Tulips!"

"Wow, look at all the colors," Felipe said.

Soon, other friends hurried into Room 26.

Slow-Down-Simon *raced* through the door, and instead

of heading to the cloakroom to hang up his jacket, he ran straight toward our table.

"Whoa! I can't believe it!" he shouted as he gazed down at the aquarium. "This is amazing!"

Felipe, Thomas, Nicole and Sophie joined him.

"Wow!" Thomas shouted. "You've got to see this!"

"Oh!" Sophie said.

"I can't believe it!" Nicole added.

Felipe just laughed.

"WHAT-WHAT-WHAT?" I squeaked as I scurried up to the tippy top of my cage to get a better look.

Soon, Mrs. Brisbane joined them. "Oh!" she said as she peered into the aquarium. "Oh, that's wonderful!"

They all stared at the aquarium.

I stared, too. Instead of two specks stuck in some strange gel, I saw two specks *swimming*.

"Og, can you see?" I squeaked.

Og was still strangely silent. I hoped he wasn't sick with some kind of frog flu.

More of my classmates gathered around the aquarium. Mrs. Brisbane made sure they all got a good look at the swimming specks.

"Oh!" Calm-Down-Cassie said. "Oh, I've never seen anything so—oh—oh!"

I noticed that her hands were shaking.

"It *is* something to see, Cassie," Mrs. Brisbane said.

I had to admit, swimming specks were more interesting than specks sitting in goo. But were they really *that* interesting?

Joey thought they were. While my friends rushed out for recess, he asked Mrs. Brisbane if he could stay inside and sketch.

"I want to draw the tadpoles at every stage," he said. "I want to get my drawings just right."

Mrs. Brisbane smiled. "Everybody is supposed to go outside at recess. Mrs. Wright wouldn't like it if you stayed inside."

Joey looked SO-SO-SO disappointed.

"Maybe just this once, she won't notice," Mrs. Brisbane said. "Go ahead and sketch."

Joey worked really hard. He'd look at the swimming specks and then back at his drawing.

"Good work, Joey!" I squeaked.

Joey didn't look up, but he said, "I want to get it just right, Humphrey. Understand?"

Of course I understood. I hoped his drawing would help me see what everyone was so excited about.

As the day went on, I realized that all my human friends thought the specks were unsqueakably interesting.

So interesting that Principal Morales came in to see them after lunch. "Amazing," he said.

I was getting a little tired of that word.

"To think that Og started out like this," he said.

Everyone looked over at my neighbor, including me.

Og just sat there on his rock, silent.

When Mr. Morales left, Mrs. Brisbane led my classmates to the library to learn more about tadpoles.

Once we were alone in the classroom, I jiggled my

lock-that-doesn't-lock and ran over to Og's tank. "Og, did you see the specks swimming?" I asked. "Mrs. Brisbane says they'll be frogs like you. Does that make you happy?"

Og didn't answer, but he stood up and dived into the water side of his tank with a gigantic *splash!*

Had the specks made him speechless?

I returned to my cage and started spinning on my wheel. That's what I do when I need to think.

Suddenly, I realized that swimming was what Og did when he wanted to think.

We both had a lot to think about.

HUMPHREY'S SPRING THINGS
Og's a good friend, loyal and true,
But do we need another TWO?

Test Trouble

⌇⌇⌇⌇⌇⌇⌇⌇⌇⌇⌇⌇⌇⌇⌇⌇⌇⌇⌇⌇⌇⌇⌇⌇⌇⌇⌇⌇⌇⌇⌇⌇⌇⌇

Late in the afternoon, Mrs. Brisbane said, "Class, it's time for us to think about Family Fun Night. We had a meeting about it yesterday and I found out that the theme is 'Circus Night.' Each class is supposed to come up with a circus-themed game or activity."

Tell-the-Truth-Thomas waved his hand and Mrs. Brisbane called on him.

"I think we should string a rope across the gym and all do tightrope walking," he said.

"Do you know how to walk a tightrope?" Mrs. Brisbane asked.

"No," Thomas answered. "But I'd like to try it. Or fly on a trapeze."

"Not me!" Calm-Down-Cassie exclaimed. "Those sound dangerous."

Mrs. Brisbane nodded. "They sound dangerous to me, too. Let's think of other circus activities."

"Clowns!" Rolling-Rosie shouted. "We can all be clowns!"

Other classmates agreed that her idea was GREAT-GREAT-GREAT.

Mrs. Brisbane nodded, but then she said, "I know that would be fun. But Ms. Mac already signed her class up to be clowns."

My classmates groaned. I was disappointed, too.

"Juggling," Small-Paul said. "We could teach people to juggle."

"Are you good at juggling?" Mrs. Brisbane asked.

"No," Small-Paul said. "But I'd like to learn."

Stop-Talking-Sophie waved her hand. "My dad can juggle. He can juggle three balls really fast and never drop them. He can even juggle knives!"

"I'm not sure about knives, but I think we'd all like to see him juggling, Sophie. Let's keep on thinking," Mrs. Brisbane continued. "We have some time to figure it out."

～✑～

I kept on thinking long after my friends had left Room 26 for the day.

Once Longfellow School was empty, I opened my lock-that-doesn't-lock and hurried out of the room to visit Gigi. If I wanted to swing up to her table to see her, I'd have to get there before Aldo closed the blinds.

"Hello, friend!" I greeted her as I slid under the door of Room 12.

"Humphrey!" she answered. "I was hoping you'd come. I have some questions."

I swung my way up to the table and hurried over to her cage. It was still light outside, so I could see her better than I could during the winter. I was very impressed with her dark brown fur coat. It wasn't golden, but it was SHINY-SHINY-SHINY.

"Did you hear about Family Fun Night?" she asked. "We're going to be clowns."

"I know," I answered. "My friends were disappointed. They wanted to be clowns, too."

Gigi shook her head. "I don't think I'll make a very good clown."

"Of course you will," I said. "Just act silly."

Gigi was silent before she finally said, "I'm not sure guinea pigs are silly."

I wasn't sure, either. "Ms. Mac will help you. She always does."

Gigi cheered up a little. "That's right. She'll help. What is your classroom doing?"

I explained that we were still trying to decide. "But I wanted to tell you about our signs of spring," I said.

Gigi listened carefully as I told her about the specks who were now swimming.

"Wow," she said. "They sound strange and amazing."

Amazing. There was that word again.

"I'm worried about Og," I explained. "He's so quiet."

"Maybe he's remembering when *he* was a tadpole. Maybe he had tadpole brothers and sisters that he misses," Gigi suggested.

I hadn't thought about that at all. She might be young, but Gigi was pretty smart!

The sun was beginning to set and I knew that Gigi was ready to go to bed. Also, Aldo would start his cleaning rounds soon, and the last thing I wanted was to be caught outside of my cage.

"You've been very helpful!" I told Gigi as I slid down the table leg and raced toward the door. "Thanks!"

"Thank you, Humphrey," she answered. "Come back soon!"

When I returned to Room 26, I told Og about my visit to see Gigi, but he was still unusually quiet.

Before I opened my cage door, I glanced at the swimming specks.

"Good night, specks," I said.

The next day, Joey told the class, "I've been reading the book that came with the tadpoles. They have breathing gills, like fish, but skin will grow over them. And then, after a while, they'll grow legs." He held up a bag. "These tadpoles came with food. But if they were living in a pond, they would eat algae."

"Ewww!" Kelsey said.

"It's natural," Joey said. "I don't think it's 'ewww.' It's kind of wonderful."

"I agree, Joey," Mrs. Brisbane said.

I heard a groan from across the room.

"What is it, Nicole?" Mrs. Brisbane asked.

"I want to see their legs today!" Nicole complained.

Nicole doesn't like to wait. I guess that's why I call her Not-Now-Nicole.

"But it will be fascinating to watch each stage," Mrs. Brisbane said.

My teacher was almost always right, but this time I wasn't sure.

⁓

When Aldo turned on the lights that night, he was strangely quiet.

He didn't say, "Never fear, 'cause Aldo's here!" or "How are you, my favorite friends?"

He just pushed his cart into the room and started sweeping.

Once, he stopped to yawn—loudly.

"Sorry, guys. I've been studying for two tests tomorrow. These are the big ones," he said. "And I have a history paper due."

"You can do it, Aldo!" I said.

He laughed. "Thanks for the encouragement, Humphrey!"

I looked over at the tadpoles swimming round and round in circles until my tummy started to hurt.

Aldo swept faster and faster, but he suddenly stopped when he reached Mrs. Brisbane's desk.

"What's this?" he said as he stared at the desktop.

"WHAT-WHAT-WHAT?" I squeaked.

Aldo picked up an envelope. "It has my name on it."

He had a puzzled look on his face as he opened the envelope and took out a piece of paper. He stared at it for a few seconds.

Then he said, "Wow!"

"What's the 'wow'?" I asked.

"Thank you, Mrs. Brisbane," he said.

He stared at the paper some more and shook his head. "Wow."

After a while, he came over to our table and said, "I just want you to know that Mrs. Brisbane is the nicest human being on earth!"

"I couldn't agree more," I squeaked.

Aldo was smiling as he left.

I was happy for him but sorry that he'd taken the piece of paper with him. I had no idea what Mrs. Brisbane had written!

～•～

Much later, after Aldo's car left the parking lot, I took out my notebook and tried to think about circus activities for Family Fun Night.

I thought and thought, but I didn't write anything down. I was still thinking about the envelope Mrs. Brisbane had left for Aldo.

"Og?" I asked my neighbor. "Do you know anything about circuses?"

Actually, I was surprised when he replied with a loud "BOING!"

It was the first sound I'd heard coming from him in days. At least he hadn't lost his voice.

"I think there are funny people dressed as clowns," I said. "And maybe tightrope walkers. But what else?"

Og dived off a rock into the water side of his tank and began to splash.

"Animals," I said. "I think animals perform. Like elephants and tigers and leopards . . ."

I stopped cold and glanced at the aquarium. Joey had told me the specks would turn into leopard frogs.

"Oh," I said. "Og, do you remember? The specks—I mean tadpoles—will be leopard frogs?"

Og splashed like crazy. I raced to the far side of my cage to avoid the water. Hamsters don't like to be wet!

"But you'll still be the only green frog in Room Twenty-six," I squeaked.

The splashing didn't stop.

Mrs. Brisbane had told us that Og was a green frog called *Rana clamitans*. It was a fancy name for a plain old frog, I thought.

"Of course, I think green frogs are the nicest," I said. "Just wanted to let you know."

Og stopped splashing and floated in the water. At least he'd calmed down.

"I'm sure our friends will come up with GREAT-GREAT-GREAT ideas for Family Fun Night," I said. "They are unsqueakably smart."

"BOING!" he agreed. It was the first time he'd agreed with me in a while.

Since Og seemed calmer, I opened my lock-that-doesn't-lock and scurried over to his tank.

"Og, do you remember being a tadpole?" I asked. It was a very personal question, but I needed to know.

Og didn't answer. Not a BOING, not a splash. He didn't even look at me. He acted very strangely—even for him.

"What's wrong?" I asked. "I'm worried about you."

62

I think he nodded his head a little bit.

"Look," I squeaked. "It doesn't bother me that you were once a tadpole. It doesn't bother me at all."

I crossed my toes because what I said wasn't exactly true.

"Like Joey said, it's kind of wonderful," I added, even though I still wasn't sure about that. I crossed my toes harder.

"BOING," Og replied.

He didn't make another sound the whole night.

In the morning, all my friends entered Room 26 and ran straight to the aquarium to see if the tadpoles had grown.

Slow-Down-Simon groaned when he got there. "They haven't changed a bit!"

"It's going to take a while," Joey reminded him.

Simon groaned again.

Only one student didn't look at the tadpoles: Calm-Down-Cassie. She went right to her chair and stared down at the top of her table.

Once class began, Mrs. Brisbane said, "I know you all studied last night, so why don't we take the math test now and get it out of the way?"

There were groans. There always were when our teacher said the word *test*.

"Now?" Do-It-Now-Daniel asked.

Mrs. Brisbane smiled nicely and said, "Yes."

Soon, my friends were bent over their papers, scribbling away. All except for Cassie.

She stared at the paper with her arms wrapped around her middle.

Cassie stared and stared, but she didn't even pick up her pencil.

Mrs. Brisbane noticed, and she walked to Cassie's desk. "Is something wrong?" she asked.

Cassie didn't look up. She mumbled something about her stomach hurting.

Mrs. Brisbane leaned down and whispered something I couldn't hear. Cassie shook her head. I thought she might even cry.

Our teacher told Cassie to go to the nurse's office, where she could lie down.

As soon as she left, Stop-Talking-Sophie asked, "Where's she going?"

Mrs. Brisbane explained that Cassie didn't feel well.

"She never feels well when we take a test," Daniel grumbled. Then he grabbed his stomach and said, "Ohhhh, my stomach."

"That's enough, Daniel," Mrs. Brisbane said. "I'll speak to you later. Now, *no more talking* during the test."

I hopped on my wheel and started to spin.

While my friends finished the test, I thought about what Daniel had said. It wasn't a kind thing to say. But to squeak the truth, Cassie had asked to go to the nurse's office the last two times the class took tests.

I don't get to take math tests unless Mrs. Brisbane writes the problems on the board. Then I copy them into my notebook and work out the answers once school is over. I've taken spelling tests and vocabulary quizzes, but they've never made me sick.

So why did tests make Cassie's tummy hurt?

When the test was over and the bell rang for recess, all of my classmates raced out of Room 26 except for Daniel. Mrs. Brisbane asked him to stay.

"That was a very rude thing to say about Cassie," Mrs. Brisbane told him.

"But it's true," Daniel said. "She just says her stomach hurts to get out of taking tests."

"You don't know that," Mrs. Brisbane said. "Some people get very anxious about taking tests and that might make her stomach hurt. But, Daniel, it's none of your business. Cassie and I will discuss it in private."

"Okay," Daniel said. "I won't say anything again."

"Thanks," Mrs. Brisbane replied. "I expect you to keep your word."

She excused him and he hurried out the door.

It wasn't long before Cassie returned to Room 26.

"Feeling better?" Mrs. Brisbane asked.

Cassie whispered, "A little bit."

Mrs. Brisbane asked her to sit down. "I'm going to call your parents and suggest that they take you to the doctor to make sure nothing's wrong," she said. "You might be sick, but since your stomach only seems to hurt when you take a test, maybe you worry about them a lot."

Cassie admitted that tests made her nervous and made her stomach feel like it was tied in knots.

"If that's the case, we need to work on ways to make you less worried about tests," Mrs. Brisbane said. "Your grades are fine. You know the material. Why do you worry so much?"

Cassie hung her head and softly said, "It's just . . . I don't want to disappoint my parents."

"I don't think you'd disappoint them if you got a few answers wrong now and then," Mrs. Brisbane said. "They'd still love you, don't you think?"

Cassie slowly nodded.

"Sometimes we learn more from our mistakes than our successes," Mrs. Brisbane suggested.

I'd certainly learned what *not* to do with the blinds cord when I made a mistake!

Then Mrs. Brisbane taught her a little trick.

"The next time you feel your stomach knotting up, take some long, slow breaths, like this." Mrs. Brisbane took a very long breath in, held it, and then slowly let the air out.

"Let's try it together," she said.

"Yes, let's!" I squeaked.

Mrs. Brisbane and Cassie tried the breathing together . . . and I did, too.

"Breathe in slowly," Mrs. Brisbane said. "Hold . . . and slowly breathe out."

I was amazed that I felt relaxed and calm after a couple of breaths.

"Does that make you feel a little better?" Mrs. Brisbane asked.

"Yes!" I squeaked.

Cassie nodded.

"Why don't you stay in for afternoon recess and take the test?" Mrs. Brisbane suggested. "You might feel calmer if the other students aren't here."

<hr />

Cassie did a lot of deep breathing as she took the test later in the day.

I breathed along with her, just to help her feel better.

I felt better, too.

"I hope it wasn't as bad as you'd expected," Mrs. Brisbane said when Cassie turned in her test.

"It wasn't," Cassie said.

And then she smiled. Whew!

HUMPHREY'S SPRING THINGS
Spring's full of flowers and all the rest,
But spring can also put you to the test!

The Big Break

~~~~~~~~~~~~~~~~~~~~~~~~~~~~~~~~~~~~

You'd think, by now, my job as a classroom hamster would have taught me what to expect in the classroom. But still, I was often caught off guard by humans and their behavior.

Especially that Friday.

Friday is always the day of the week when I go home with one of my classmates for the weekend. I have FUN-FUN-FUN, and I get to learn even more about my human friends.

But instead of revealing who would take me home for the weekend, Mrs. Brisbane made a surprising announcement.

"Class, I'm going to be taking Humphrey and Og home for spring break. Joey is taking the tadpoles to his house for the week," she said.

"The *week?*" I squeaked. "Don't you mean the *weekend?*"

"I'm not giving you any homework over spring break," she continued. "But I want you to bring in more signs of spring. I think you'll find a lot of them. And when we get back, we'll make a plan for Family Fun Night and start a great new project."

"I still like the tightrope idea," Tell-the-Truth-Thomas said. "I might even try it over spring break."

Some of my friends laughed, but not me.

"I can't figure out why they call it spring break," I squeaked. "What's broken about spring?"

No one answered. My friends seemed extra excited for the bell to ring at the end of the day, but I was extra confused.

Don't get me wrong. I LOVE-LOVE-LOVE going home with Mrs. Brisbane and spending time with her and her husband, Bert. And it's NICE-NICE-NICE that Og would get to come with me. I thought he needed a break from the specks—I mean tadpoles. But I wondered what my friends would do over spring break.

Even more, I wondered what would happen with Joey's tadpoles. Would they grow legs and arms and heads?

Up to now, I hadn't seen much progress.

It didn't matter what I wondered, because at the end of the day, Mrs. Brisbane brought my cage out to her car. Mr. Morales carried out Og's tank.

"Sue, you are a wonder," he said. "Caring for all of these animals takes a lot of work, but the children get so much out of having them in the classroom."

I guess it does take a lot of work to care for animals. But as a classroom pet, let me say that it takes a lot of work to care for humans, too.

In the end, all the work pays off, because I help my friends and they help me.

~⚬~

I like Mrs. Brisbane's house. It's painted a cheery shade of yellow—almost the color of a Golden Hamster like me—and has white shutters.

Inside, she always has fresh flowers on the table—even when it's not spring.

"Bert, our houseguests are here!" she announced as she carried my cage through the front door.

Mr. Brisbane rolled his wheelchair to the door and she put my cage in his lap.

"Welcome back, Humphrey," he said. "You're just what we need for spring break."

"Thanks!" I squeaked.

After he put my cage on the large table in the living room, Mrs. Brisbane said, "Let's get Og out of the car."

Mr. Brisbane rolled his chair outside, and when he came back, he had Og's tank on his lap. He and Mrs. Brisbane set it on the table next to me.

"They're used to being together all the time," she said.

Mr. Brisbane nodded. "It's hard to understand, but somehow, this hamster and this frog are truly friends."

He is a very wise man. But recently, I was having trouble connecting with my friend Og.

Maybe a week at the Brisbanes' house would help.

"What are your plans for the week?" Bert asked his wife.

70

"Oh, I hope to sleep late every day," she said.

Really? I couldn't imagine Mrs. Brisbane sleeping late.

"I'll have lunch with my friends and clean out a closet or two," she continued. "But I also have to catch up on work."

Mr. Brisbane took her hand. "Do you have to, Sue?"

Mrs. Brisbane sighed. "I really need to figure out what our class is doing for Family Fun Night. The theme this year is the circus, and I don't have a clue."

Mr. Brisbane thought for a moment. "You could be clowns!"

"We thought of that," Mrs. Brisbane said. "But Morgan already signed her class up for that."

Morgan is Ms. Mac's first name. Morgan McNamara. My first teacher!

Mr. Brisbane patted his wife's hand. "We'll think of something," he said.

"I HOPE-HOPE-HOPE so," I squeaked.

The Brisbanes both chuckled.

"If I could only understand him," Mrs. Brisbane said. "I think I would learn a lot."

I have to admit, I think she was right!

While the Brisbanes ate dinner, I talked to Og. "Do you know what?" I asked. "I just thought of something."

He replied with a single "BOING."

"You know how a circus has all kinds of animal acts?" As soon as I squeaked "animal acts," my whiskers began to wiggle. "They're mostly large and fearsome creatures

71

like lions and tigers and elephants. Some of them jump through hoops. Not the elephants, of course."

"BOING-BOING," Og twanged. He had a lot more to say now than he did when the specks were swimming nearby.

"And people do tricks on horseback," I added.

"BOING?" Og replied.

"Humans love them," I said. "And I know a couple of other animals that humans *love* to watch."

After dinner, the Brisbanes came back to the living room.

"Anything on TV?" Bert asked.

"Not really," Mrs. Brisbane replied. "Let's talk about the circus."

Mr. Brisbane leaned back and stared at the ceiling for a moment. "I haven't been to the circus for years," he said. "Not since Jason was a boy."

Jason was the Brisbanes' grown-up son, who lived FAR-FAR-FAR away. I'd never thought about Mr. Brisbane taking his young son to the circus.

I'd never thought about the Brisbanes being like the families of my classmates.

"He really loved the strong man, who lifted—oh, I can't remember—something like two or three times his own weight," Bert said.

"Eeek!" I squeaked.

"And there was the human cannonball," Mrs. Brisbane said. "I saw that once when I was a girl. The man flew out of the cannon and landed in a net."

"EEEK-EEEK-EEEK!" I squeaked.

Mr. Brisbane laughed. "I don't think you'll be shooting your students out of a cannon or having them lift things twice their weights."

"The parents might get upset," Mrs. Brisbane said, giggling.

I'd never heard her giggle in Room 26.

They were silent for a while, thinking about circus acts.

"Sophie's dad can juggle," she said. "Oh, I really don't have any ideas at all."

"Animal acts!" I squeaked.

No one paid the least attention to me, except Og.

"BOING!" he shouted.

Still, the Brisbanes were silent as they thought.

"I'll show them, Og," I told my friend. I scrambled up my tree branch to the tippy top of my cage.

"Goodness," Mrs. Brisbane said. "Humphrey is energetic tonight."

I reached up to the top bars of my cage and began swinging my way from one to another.

"Look at him go," Mrs. Brisbane said. "I'd like to see Humphrey on a trapeze."

When I got to the far corner of the cage, I held my breath and let go, dropping all the way to the bottom. Thank goodness for the layer of soft bedding there. It was like falling onto a pillow.

I quickly leaped onto my wheel and began spinning as fast as I could.

Luckily, the Brisbanes noticed.

"Look at him go!" Mr. Brisbane said. "He's amazing!"

Up until then, I had not liked the word *amazing* when it was used to describe two swimming specks. But I liked the idea that maybe I was amazing, too.

Mrs. Brisbane sat up and stared at me. "Bert, circuses have animal acts!"

"Of course," he said. "But I don't think you'll be bringing an elephant to Longfellow School."

"We have our own animals," she said. "The families could do something that has to do with hamsters and frogs."

"Spin a wheel like Humphrey?" Mr. Brisbane said.

His wife nodded. "Run a maze."

Just then, Og made a spectacular leap into the water side of his tank.

"A water tank?" Mrs. Brisbane asked.

"Leapfrog," Mr. Brisbane said.

Suddenly, they both laughed. I laughed, too, at the thought of frogs leaping over each other.

"I think we're on to something," Mrs. Brisbane said.

Bert nodded. "Thanks to Humphrey and Og . . . as always."

"You're welcome!" I squeaked.

I didn't sleep much that night. I was too busy thinking about animal acts for the circus.

I knew that Og and I couldn't do what the horses and

elephants did. But still . . . we could help our human friends if we just found a way.

Mrs. Brisbane slept late on Saturday and spent the rest of the day cleaning out a closet and filling boxes with clothes and books and all kinds of things to give away. She called it "spring cleaning."

Bert cleaned out his closet as well.

"What about the circus?" I squeaked when they both settled down in the living room for a cup of tea after dinner.

"Humphrey, you're always telling us what to do," Mrs. Brisbane said. "If we could only understand you."

"I do have great ideas sometimes," I said. "I wish you could understand me, too!"

I was never completely sure whether Og could understand me, either, but he chimed in with a very loud "BOING!"

The Brisbanes both laughed long and hard.

"I wish they could come here every weekend," Mr. Brisbane said.

Mrs. Brisbane nodded. "But my students get so much out of having Humphrey come home with them."

It was true. I was a big help to my fellow students. But I wanted to help my teacher as well.

"I have some new thoughts about the circus acts," Mr. Brisbane said. "You'll need a ringmaster. Or ring-mistress."

"GOOD-GOOD-GOOD!" I exclaimed.

Mrs. Brisbane yawned loudly. "Good idea, Bert," she said. "But right now I just want to get some sleep."

"Tomorrow," Mr. Brisbane said.

"Tomorrow," Mrs. Brisbane agreed.

They headed toward the bedroom.

"Og," I squeaked to my friend. "It sounds like we'll have to wait until tomorrow to find out what Room Twenty-six is doing for Family Fun Night."

"BOING," he said.

It was a very disappointed "BOING."

HUMPHREY'S SPRING THINGS

Spring break is fun—that's a fact.
But will we come up with a circus act?

A Change of Plans

The Brisbanes' house was calm and cozy. I slept a lot more there than I do in Room 26. I guess maybe I needed a spring break just like everybody else!

Early in the week, Mrs. Brisbane got a call from Cassie's mom.

I knew that because I could hear Mrs. Brisbane say, "Thanks for calling me back. How is Cassie?" And, "I'm glad the doctor said she's fine."

That was GOOD-GOOD-GOOD news.

Mrs. Brisbane listened for a while. Then she said, "If you're free, would you like to come over here so we could talk?" She paused and then said, "Yes, of course, bring Cassie. I think Humphrey and Og could use some company."

As much as I love the Brisbanes, it was true. I missed my classmates. After all, I am a classroom pet.

Later in the day, the doorbell rang. Mrs. Brisbane led Cassie and her mom into the living room.

I leaped up and squeaked, "HI-HI-HI, Cassie!"

Even Og splashed around in the water side of his tank. "BOING-BOING-BOING!" he shouted.

Cassie raced over to see us. She looked unsqueakably happy, as if her stomach didn't hurt at all. She asked if she could put me in my hamster ball, and before I knew it, I was rolling around the room.

Mr. Brisbane offered them lemonade, and they all gathered around the living room table to talk.

"The doctor said that Cassie gets very anxious about tests and things like that," Cassie's mom said. "Cassie told me you suggested deep breathing, which I think is great."

"Does it help, Cassie?" Mrs. Brisbane asked.

"Yes," Cassie said. "But sometimes I forget."

Mrs. Brisbane nodded. "There are some other things you can try," she said. "For instance, getting plenty of exercise can help, like walking or running."

A GREAT-GREAT-GREAT idea! I always exercise when I'm feeling out of control.

To encourage Cassie, I decided to see how hard I could get my hamster ball spinning. Instead of just running forward, which makes the ball roll, I began to spin in a circle.

"Look!" Cassie said as she pointed at me.

The ball was spinning round and round in a circle.

In fact, the world around me was spinning so fast, I was a little bit dizzy!

"BOING-BOING!" Og sounded worried.

My tummy felt funny, so I stopped my spinning.

When the ball was at a standstill, I looked up and saw Cassie spinning round and round in a circle, too.

"Be careful, Cassie," her mom said.

"It's fun!" Cassie said.

She spun a little while longer and finally stopped.

"How do you feel?" Mrs. Brisbane asked.

Cassie caught her breath. "I feel good. More relaxed."

"That's good," Mrs. Brisbane said. "But maybe walking is a little better than spinning."

My head was still spinning, so I squeaked, "I think so!"

Thank goodness, Cassie put me back in my cage.

Mr. Brisbane returned to the living room with a plate of oatmeal cookies.

Cookies *always* make humans feel better.

While everyone munched away, I hopped on my wheel for a good, fast spin.

"Look!" Mrs. Brisbane said. "I think Humphrey exercises to relax."

Cassie giggled. "But he doesn't take tests."

"If you only knew!" I squeaked.

Mr. Brisbane passed the cookies around again. "When I was in school, I always thought I had to get every single answer right. If I missed just one question, I thought I'd failed." He chuckled. "But now I know that you don't have to be perfect all the time."

"I worry about missing an answer, too," Cassie said.

Mr. Brisbane nodded. "But would the world come to an end if you got an answer wrong now and then?"

Cassie hesitated, then shook her head. "I guess not."

"Of course not, Cassie," her mom said. "You could never disappoint us. We know you try hard and we're proud of what a good person you are."

They hugged, which is something nice that humans

do. But PLEASE-PLEASE-PLEASE don't hug your hamsters. We could get hurt!

"You don't have to be perfect, Cassie. Relax," her mom said.

"I know." Cassie sighed.

"There's something you can do about that," Mrs. Brisbane said. "Whenever you have a negative thought—such as thinking you're going to fail—replace it with a positive thought."

Cassie looked confused.

"When you hear that voice in your head saying that you're going to fail, just say to yourself, 'I know I'll do well on the test,'" Mrs. Brisbane said. "Because you know you are prepared."

"That's a good idea, isn't it, Og?" I squeaked to my neighbor.

"BOING-BOING," he replied.

Suddenly, Cassie smiled. "I guess I could do that. Because I always study a lot."

Her mom smiled, too. "Try following Mrs. Brisbane's suggestions. Maybe your stomach won't hurt so much."

"I'm going to try those things, too!" I squeaked. "I'm going to breathe deeply, get plenty of exercise and replace my negative thoughts with positive ones!"

I suddenly felt lighter than air. I scrambled up the tree branch, grabbed the top rungs of my cage and started swinging my way from one corner to the next.

"Look at Humphrey!" Cassie laughed.

"He's quite a show-off," Mrs. Brisbane said.

A show-off? Not me! I was just following Mrs. Brisbane's suggestions.

Cassie came over to my cage to watch. "I love you, Humphrey," she said. "You're so funny!"

"Thanks!" I squeaked as I dropped down to the bottom of my cage and did a triple somersault.

Cassie laughed out loud. "I hope you can come home with me sometime," she said.

As I hopped onto my wheel and began to spin, I heard Mrs. Brisbane say something I didn't expect.

"Would you like to take him home now?" she asked. "Over spring break?"

Cassie was speechless. I was squeakless.

"What do you think?" Cassie's mom asked.

"Oh, yes," Cassie said in a soft voice. "I would love that."

"I think Humphrey would love that, too," she said.

I was still squeakless. I'd planned on spending a nice, quiet week with the Brisbanes and Og. Suddenly, that wasn't going to happen!

"Do you know how to take care of him?" Mrs. Brisbane asked. "I have some instructions you can take with you."

Cassie's hands were shaking.

"It's a big responsibility," her mom said.

"I want to," Cassie said. "More than anything! Can Og come with us?"

Og hopped up and down. "BOING-BOING!" he said.

I think he wanted to go home with Cassie, too.

"Well, Mr. Brisbane and I would be very lonely without one of the classroom pets," she said. "Let's share."

Cassie nodded, and before I knew it, her mom carried my cage out to the car. I barely had time to squeak, "So long, Og!" on my way out.

I did hear a distant "BOING!"

All of my friends are excited when I come visit their homes. So am I.

But I don't think anyone was ever as excited to take me home as Cassie was.

She was so excited, she was swinging my cage a little too much for my wobbly tummy, but I understood.

"Where should I put him?" she asked as she carried my cage through the door.

"In your room, I think," her mom said.

"I hope I can take good care of him." Cassie set my cage on her desk.

"You will," her mom said.

"You'll do a hamster-iffic job," I squeaked.

Cassie got right to work, filling my water bottle and smoothing out my bedding. She straightened my wheel and gave me some vitamin drops, which are yummy!

Later that night, her older sister, Cammy, came in to watch me spin on my wheel.

"I need to exercise, too," Cassie said as she ran in place.

Cammy joined her, and pretty soon, the whole room was shaking!

After dinner, Cassie got into her pajamas and came back to her room.

"Would you like me to read you a story?" she asked. "I love reading stories."

I didn't know that, but I enjoyed listening to her read from her fairy-tale books. The first story was about a little girl who was no bigger than a thumb.

As a tiny hamster, I could understand how unsqueak-ably scary it can be to be so small, but it had a happy ending.

Then she read a more disturbing story about a frog prince. A princess doesn't realize that the frog is a real prince until she finally kisses him and he turns back into a prince.

"Isn't that a happy ending?" Cassie asked as she closed the book.

I had nothing to say. The thought that Og could be a prince or that a princess would kiss him was—um— disturbing.

"I love happy endings," Cassie said.

Just then, her mom popped her head in the door. "Time to go to sleep," she said. "Did you brush your teeth?"

"I did," Cassie said.

Cassie's mom tucked her into bed and turned out the light.

"I'm so happy to have Humphrey here, I'm not sure if I can sleep," she said.

Her mom suggested she try the breathing exercise Mrs. Brisbane had taught her.

Once we were alone, I heard Cassie say, "Come on, Humphrey. Let's breathe."

Actually, I breathe all the time. But that night, we did it together.

"Breathe in slowly," she said. "Hold . . . and slowly breathe out."

We repeated that several times, but after a while, I didn't hear Cassie anymore.

I was sound asleep.

I think maybe she was, too.

HUMPHREY'S SPRING THINGS
We breathe in and out all through the day,
But breathing like this makes worries float away!

Spectacular Signs of Spring

~•~•~•~•~•~•~•~•~•~•~•~•~•~•~•~•~•~

Spring *almost* ruined my week at Cassie's house.

Don't get me wrong; she took excellent care of me. She even took me out of my cage, which I enjoy, especially when my friends make mazes for me to run.

But Cassie was also WORRIED-WORRIED-WORRIED about finding signs of spring.

And as the week went on, she got more and more worried.

"Do some deep breathing," her mom said when Cassie moaned that she couldn't find one new thing to add to her list.

"I'm busy," Cammy said when Cassie begged her to help.

Cassie's dad took her to the park one day. They were gone for hours, but when she came back, she was almost in tears.

"Sure, the grass is starting to turn green and the trees have buds on them. But they're *already on the list*! Mrs. Brisbane will be so upset if I can't find something," she said.

"I thought Mrs. Brisbane was your favorite teacher ever," her dad said. "She'll understand."

But Cassie was still upset.

The next day, Cassie's mom took her for a long walk around the neighborhood. I crossed my toes and hoped that the exercise would calm her down.

I spent the day in my cage, napping, spinning on my wheel and staring out the window. I missed Og. I missed my classmates. I even missed the specks!

That afternoon, while I was thinking about them and looking out the window, I noticed something new.

A small brown bird lit on a tree branch and then hopped a few inches, just out of my view.

I climbed to the top of my cage. I could see it!

The bird hopped farther until I couldn't see it again. So I scurried over to the corner and stretched my neck. The bird was standing on the edge of a nest. A smaller brown bird was inside the nest.

My neck was getting tired, but I kept staring at the nest. It was woven out of twigs, bits of mud, fluff, paper and straw.

It was a wonderful sight! And birds' nests are definitely signs of spring.

I couldn't wait for Cassie to come back from her walk so she could see it, too.

When she returned, she looked VERY-VERY-VERY discouraged as she slumped down on her bed.

"Nothing new," she said. "The signs of spring have stopped."

I raced to the front of my cage and squeaked, "NO-NO-NO! There is a birds' nest right outside the window. Look!"

I tried to point, but since Cassie wasn't looking at me, it didn't matter.

She sighed. "I'll be the only one in Room Twenty-six without a new sign of spring."

"Look outside! At the very edge of the window!" I squeaked at the top of my lungs.

Cassie didn't notice. As wonderful as they are, humans can be very frustrating at times.

In fact, I was so frustrated that I jumped up and down. "Please look!"

Cassie glanced over at me and smiled. "Oh, Humphrey, you're so cute."

Cute? I don't care about being cute! (Okay, maybe a little bit.)

To squeak the truth, I was a little bit upset with Cassie until I realized that from where she was sitting, she couldn't see the tree branch. The curtain was blocking her view.

"Pull back the curtain!" I squeaked. "It's right outside the window."

Cassie just sighed.

Of course, once it was dark outside, there was no chance of Cassie seeing the nest.

She left the room to have dinner and watch television with her family.

As she did, I began to think.

Squeaking at Cassie wasn't helping at all, since she couldn't understand me. I needed to show her the nest—but how?

Later, Cassie came back to her room for bedtime. She read for a while before her dad turned off the light.

"I hope you're not too disappointed in me, Humphrey," Cassie said.

Then her breathing changed and I could tell that she was asleep.

Her mom had closed the curtain completely when she said good night to Cassie, but there was a little opening that let some moonlight in.

I stared at the moonlight a long time before I came up with a Plan.

I waited until the house was completely quiet, and then I carefully jiggled the lock-that-doesn't-lock on my cage and tiptoed out onto the table.

There was only about an inch of space between the table and the windowsill.

I held my breath and leaped.

Whew! I was pawsitively relieved to land safely.

I stopped to catch my breath, then I began to push the curtain away from the window.

I had no idea that a curtain could be so heavy. I pushed with all my might, and nothing happened.

Whoa! I took a deep breath, pushed again, and the

curtain slowly began to move. The great thing about those curtains was that when I pushed the left curtain, the right curtain also moved.

With a few deep breaths, and a few rest stops, I managed to push the curtain as far as it would go.

Once I caught my breath, I stopped to look at the moon. And then I looked down. The silvery light was shining on the nest tucked in the branches of the tree. I was closer now and could see much better.

I stared for a while, because it was so round and cozy. Almost as cozy as my little sleeping hut.

I crossed my toes and HOPED-HOPED-HOPED that in the morning, Cassie would see the nest, too.

By the time I returned to my cage and closed the door behind me, I was feeling unsqueakably tired.

I sank down into my bedding and stared up at the moon until, suddenly, it was morning.

I'd slept through most of the night—which is quite a feat for a hamster!

"Good morning, Humphrey," Cassie said as she looked in my cage.

"Don't look at me—look out the window! There's a spectacular sign of spring!" I squeaked excitedly.

Cassie just yawned.

"Ready for breakfast?" her dad asked as he poked his head in the doorway. "I made pancakes and sausage and biscuits, scrambled eggs and pizza!"

"Really?" Cassie flapped her hands excitedly.

Her dad laughed. "April fools!" he said. "Didn't you look at the calendar? It's April first—April Fools' Day!"

Cassie laughed and then turned serious. "What are we really having for breakfast?"

"The good news is, we *are* having pancakes," he said with a smile.

"Yay!" Cassie raced out of the room.

Why would Cassie's dad fib about all the things he made for breakfast? Because it was April Fools' Day? Why is there a day to celebrate being foolish? I will never figure out humans!

I sighed. The cozy nest was now in plain view . . . only Cassie wasn't there to see it.

I thought of making a sign saying BIRDS' NEST with a big arrow pointing at the window. But if I did that, Cassie would know that I can read and write and get out of my cage. Those are things I like to keep secret.

Cassie and her mom came back in a little while.

"I'll make the bed if you pick up your clothes," her mom said, and they got to work.

"Please . . . look out the window!" I squeaked.

"Why is Humphrey squeaking like that?" Cassie's mom asked.

Cassie giggled. "He's talking."

"Yes!" I squeaked at the top of my small lungs. "I'm trying to tell you to LOOK OUT THE WINDOW!"

Cassie and her mom just laughed.

After they straightened up the room, Cassie's mom said, "Wow, it's really bright this morning."

I crossed my toes and hoped.

Cassie's mom walked across the room to the window. "I'll just close these a little."

"NO-NO-NO!" I screamed.

My heart sank as she started to pull the curtains together—after I'd worked so hard to open them.

And then she stopped!

"Cassie, come here," she said. "Look at that branch!"

She pointed and Cassie looked.

"I don't see anything except leaves," she said.

I held my breath.

"Look again," her mom said.

Cassie gasped and clapped her hands. "It's a nest!" she shouted as she danced around in a circle. "Oh, Mom—it's a nest!"

"Calm down, Cassie," her mom said. "You'll scare the birds away."

Cassie took a deep breath. I could tell she was trying to stay calm.

"I can't believe it," Cassie whispered. "We're so close!"

"I think you found your sign of spring," her mom said as she hurried out of the room. "I'm going to get your dad and Cammy."

I could breathe again. My Plan had worked.

For the rest of my time at Cassie's house, the whole family came to watch the birds.

"The female must be sitting on some eggs," Cassie's dad said. "Watch how the male bird brings her food."

Cammy gave Cassie tips on how to get the best photos.

Cassie's dad printed the photos out for her.

And Cassie's mom found a book in the library about how birds build nests.

"Look! There's my old pink shoelace." Cassie pointed to the nest and Cammy took a picture.

Cassie took notes, made drawings, and even made a video of the male bringing food for the female. Once in a while, she left the nest to get food and the male stayed behind.

"They're so wonderful. How can we help them?" Cassie asked her mother.

Cassie's mom had an idea. She took Cassie to the store to buy bird seed and a feeder, so it would be easier for the birds to have food.

Cassie took more pictures of the birds taking turns going to the feeder.

The birds worked hard together and helped each other. Just like Cassie's family.

I had a little pang as I thought about how wonderful families really were. I wished I had one, too.

❧

On Sunday—my last day at Cassie's—some very surprising things happened.

First of all, Cassie and Cammy took baskets and ran

through the backyard, picking up brightly colored eggs. They said the Easter Bunny had left them.

But why an Easter Bunny? Why not an Easter Hamster?

They also ate a good amount of chocolate, which they didn't share. That's a good thing, because candy isn't healthy for hamsters to eat.

The other surprising thing that happened on Sunday was that the small brown bird flew off while the father bird stood guard on the edge of the nest.

That's when we saw them: three small speckled eggs! Cassie managed to take a photo just before the mother bird returned to the nest.

I never thought the sight of three eggs could be so wonderful! Even more egg-citing than the eggs left by the Easter Bunny.

"I can't wait for school tomorrow," Cassie told me that night. "I'll have the best signs of spring in Room Twenty-six."

"I think you're right," I squeaked.

~⁓~

When class began on Monday morning, Cassie ran up to Mrs. Brisbane and asked, "Are we going to share our signs of spring this morning?"

"Yes," Mrs. Brisbane said. "Did you find some?"

Cassie nodded. "I found something wonderful."

Our teacher smiled and told Cassie to take her seat.

Tell-the-Truth-Thomas entered with a shocked look on his face. "It's starting to snow!" he said.

Mrs. Brisbane looked surprised.

I looked out the window and saw that it was a beautiful, sunny spring day.

Suddenly, Thomas grinned. "April fools!"

Mrs. Brisbane smiled and said, "This isn't April first, Thomas."

"I know," Thomas said. "But we were on break for April Fools' Day, so I had to do it today."

Just before the bell rang, Joey arrived, carrying the aquarium. It was covered with a cloth, so I couldn't see inside. He walked very slowly and set it down SO-SO-SO carefully.

"Wait till you see, Og," Joey whispered.

"BOING-BOING-BOING!" Og jumped up and down on a rock.

Rosie rolled her wheelchair toward the aquarium. "Let's see!"

"Not now," Mrs. Brisbane said. "Joey will uncover it when we talk about our signs of spring. Right, Joey?"

Joey smiled and nodded. He looked like he had a big, happy secret.

Normally, I wouldn't change a thing Mrs. Brisbane does. But that morning, I WISHED-WISHED-WISHED she wouldn't make us study our vocabulary words first thing in the morning.

How could I think about words like *wander*, *observe* and *drift* when I *observed* that my mind was *wandering* and *drifting* to thoughts about that covered aquarium?

I think many of my friends had the same problem,

because they kept sneaking glances at our table by the window.

At last, it was time for recess and my friends all hurried out to the playground, leaving me staring at a piece of cloth. I concentrated on looking out the window instead, and I noticed the first drops of rain beginning to fall.

"I guess our students will be back soon," Mrs. Brisbane said out loud.

Suddenly, a few drops of rain turned to millions of drops of rain.

My classmates returned to Room 26 quickly, and they were dripping wet. Mrs. Brisbane gave them paper towels to dry their arms and faces.

"We still have a few minutes of recess," she said. "What would you like to do?"

"See what's in the aquarium!" Tell-the-Truth-Thomas shouted.

Everyone else loudly agreed—including me.

Even Og said, "BOING-BOING!"

Mrs. Brisbane took her chalk and stood by our signs of spring list on the board.

"What did you find over spring break?" she asked.

Holly held up a beautiful photo of a tree with white flowers. "It's a dogwood," she said.

Which was strange, because it didn't look anything like a dog.

My friends had seen pink trees and red birds and black birds.

Tall-Paul held up a large drawing of a nose.

"What's that?" Mrs. Brisbane asked.

"I have allergies in the spring," he said. "They make my nose run."

Everybody laughed, but I didn't understand. Your nose is attached to your face. How can it run? And where does it go?

"Allergies are very unpleasant signs of spring," Mrs. Brisbane agreed.

Calm-Down-Cassie waved her arm until I thought it would fall off. Mrs. Brisbane finally called on her.

"Two birds built a nest right outside my bedroom," she said. "And there are eggs!" She held up a page of photos. "I have video, too. It was the most wonderful thing I've ever seen."

"I saw it, too!" I squeaked.

Small-Paul shared his temperature chart that showed that it was continuing to get warmer and warmer.

"What about the tadpoles?" Rosie asked. "I just can't wait."

Mrs. Brisbane waited until the end to call on Joey.

"I guess it's time," Mrs. Brisbane said.

It was time, all right. Though I was a tiny bit worried about what I'd see in that tank!

HUMPHREY'S SPRING THINGS
I hadn't seen specks for all of spring break.
What kind of changes did those two make?

Uncle Og

Joey had a huge grin as he walked over to our table and stood next to the aquarium.

"It's not easy to take care of tadpoles," he said. "But I followed all of the directions and . . ." He pulled the cloth off the tank. "They have little legs now, and if you look closely, you can see their heads are changing!" Joey looked so proud, I thought he'd burst!

The rest of our classmates jumped out of their seats and rushed toward the aquarium.

Mrs. Brisbane got them to line up and calm down.

Og, however, didn't calm down one bit.

"BOING-BOING-BOING-BOING!" he twanged as he jumped up and down.

I have never seen him so excited.

Somehow, our teacher made sure my friends looked at the tank one by one.

"Fan-TAS-tic!" Thomas said.

"Oooh, see those bumps?" Rosie said. "I think that's the beginning of their arms."

Every single classmate said that the tadpoles were the

most amazing, spectacular, wonderful, awesome things they'd ever seen in their lives!

Really? Hadn't they seen me leap onto my wheel and leap off again without falling? Hadn't they seen me swing across the top of my cage?

Of course, they hadn't seen my adventures outside of my cage, but if they had, they'd think I was amazing and wonderful, too! (Not to mention the fact that I can read and write.)

Growing legs and bumpy arms? That took no work at all.

Cassie wasn't quite as excited as the other students. "That's very interesting," she said. "But have you ever seen birds build a nest?"

"I haven't," Mrs. Brisbane said. "But I'd like to. Thanks for sharing your pictures with us."

"Yes, thanks, Cassie," Helpful-Holly said. "I'd love to see the baby birds hatch."

Cassie invited Holly over to her house, and I could tell she felt a lot better.

I would have liked to see the baby birds hatch, too!

I'd been a little upset with Mrs. Brisbane for making us wait for the unveiling of the tadpoles, but I was HAPPY-HAPPY-HAPPY when she let the students take time to watch them.

Not that they did much. But they didn't look like specks anymore, and that was interesting to every-body.

I think it was especially interesting to Og.

"BOING-BOING!" he said. Then he jumped into the water to do some serious splashing.

After that, he went back to his rock and looked over at the aquarium.

"BOING-BOING-BOING-BOING!" he exclaimed in a very loud voice.

"I think Og likes them," Nicole said.

I wasn't so sure about that.

"Maybe he remembers being a tadpole, too!" Harry said.

"We should name them," Thomas suggested. "How about 'Tad' and 'Pole'?"

Some of my friends groaned at that idea.

Then Simon said, "We should call Og 'Uncle'!"

Everybody loved that idea (except maybe me).

"Uncle Og! Uncle Og!" they repeated.

"BOING-BOING!" Og joined in.

I was unsqueakably relieved when it was time for lunch and my friends had to leave the classroom.

I needed a break!

Besides, I hadn't had a chance to get a good look at the tadpoles myself.

Once the room was quiet—which it hadn't been all morning—I moved to the side of my cage closest to the aquarium and looked.

The specks were bigger and, yes, they actually did have legs.

They had round things that looked a little bit like heads, if you used your imagination.

Luckily, I have a good imagination.

Then I looked across the aquarium to see Og.

Og had a huge head. He was green. He had strong legs.

The tadpoles didn't look anything like him. So why were my friends calling him "Uncle Og"? If he was the tadpoles' uncle, was I their uncle, too?

Just because he was a frog, did that mean they were in the same family?

And where was my family, anyway?

"So, what do you think, Og?" I squeaked. "Do you like the tadpoles?"

He was completely silent, so I kept talking. "I can't believe how much they changed."

No answer.

"Do you remember being a tadpole?" I asked.

"BOING!" Og's voice boomed.

I'm not sure, but I think maybe he didn't remember.

"I don't remember being a baby hamster, either," I said. "At least I don't think I do."

After that, Og didn't make any noise at all. I wondered if he'd dozed off. You can never tell with a frog.

⁓

Later that afternoon, Mrs. Brisbane told the class that she had an idea for Family Fun Night.

"Since we have animals in our classroom, I thought

we could have fun doing animal activities for the circus," she explained.

Helpful-Holly waved her hand. "Oooh, I saw a lady in a pink dress standing on the back of a horse at the circus and they were going round and round the ring really fast!"

"Well, I don't think we'll be doing that." Mrs. Brisbane chuckled. "Mrs. Wright would not approve of horses racing around the gym."

We all laughed at the thought of that.

"I was thinking that we could have activities that have to do with hamsters and frogs," she said.

Calm-Down-Cassie waved her hand. "We made a hamster maze in the after-school program."

"We could set up a maze—like an obstacle course—and people could buy a ticket to run through it," Harry suggested. "We could time them. If they beat the clock, they get a prize."

Mrs. Brisbane nodded. "I like that idea, Harry."

Kelsey's hand shot up. "Oooh, we could have the parents and their kids do a leapfrog race."

The thought of my friends' parents leaping around like frogs was unsqueakably funny to me.

"BOING-BOING!" I guess Og liked that idea.

"And I thought we could have some of you take turns as ringmaster or ringmistress to draw people in," Mrs. Brisbane said.

"I want to do that," Rosie said.

"Great! Let's take a vote," Mrs. Brisbane said. "Who would like Room Twenty-six to sign up to do animal acts?"

Every single hand shot up. I raised my paw.

Og said, "BOING!" I don't think he can actually raise one leg at a time.

Sophie asked, "Can Humphrey and Og be in the gym, too? And the tadpoles?"

Mrs. Brisbane said, "Mrs. Wright won't like that. But I think Mr. Morales will. And after all, he is her boss. I'll see what I can do."

There were cheers and applause.

Mrs. Brisbane wasn't finished. "Since we're getting ready for Family Fun Night, I have an assignment that has to do with families and how they grow."

She asked Holly to pass around sheets of paper.

"We're all going to make family trees," she said. "A family tree shows the people who live in your family now. And it also shows your relatives from the past. You're going to build yours branch by branch."

I was confused. I may not remember my family, but I'm pretty sure they didn't grow on trees. And neither do human families.

"To start with, for your homework tonight, I want you to write your name at the bottom of the tree—there's a space for it." She continued, "And then on the lowest branch, write the name of your mother on the right side and your father on the left side."

Holly raised her hand. "You mean Janet and Steve? Those are my parents' names."

"Their full names, including your mother's maiden name," Mrs. Brisbane replied. "That's her last name from when she was a girl. Some moms keep their last name and some take their husband's."

Daniel frowned. "I have no idea what my mom's maiden name is."

"Ask her," our teacher said. "Then, I want you to draw apples hanging from the tree to show your brothers and sisters, if you have any. Write their names in the apples."

Sophie was already at work. "Timothy," she said as she wrote on her paper.

"Mrs. Brisbane, I have a half sister," Nicole said.

A half sister? I'd never heard of such a thing! Which half was she?

"My mom and dad got divorced," she continued. "My mom married my stepdad, and they had my sister. Where do I put her?"

Oh! So that's what a half sister is.

"Make an apple on the tree for her. All kinds of sisters and brothers should be included," Mrs. Brisbane said. "You don't have to do it now. Bring it in tomorrow."

As usual, I didn't get a sheet, so I wasn't sure what a family tree looked like *or* why brothers and sisters were apples!

My friends raced out of the room, but Thomas hung back with a worried look on his face.

"Mrs. Brisbane," he said when all of the students were gone, "I don't know what to put on my tree because I'm adopted."

"That doesn't make any difference," she said. "Do you live with someone that you call Mom or Dad?"

Thomas nodded. "Both."

"And do you love them and they love you back?" she asked.

Thomas nodded again.

"Then those are your parents," Mrs. Brisbane said. "The people who love you and take care of you. Write their names on the family tree."

"Okay," Thomas said.

I wasn't sure what *that* was all about, so I hopped on my wheel for a good, long spin to try and figure things out.

~·~

After my spin, I crawled into my sleeping hut, and by the time I woke up, it was dark outside.

It was too late to visit Gigi, even though I wanted to tell her about our Family Fun Night plans.

Og was quiet, so I sat and waited for Aldo to arrive. I was eager to see what he thought of the tadpoles. They were quiet, too.

Suddenly, the door opened and the lights came on.

"Greetings, Aldo!" I squeaked. After all, I hadn't seen my friend for more than a week.

I was SHOCKED-SHOCKED-SHOCKED to see that the person pulling his cleaning cart into Room 26 wasn't Aldo at all. It was a complete stranger!

"You're not Aldo!" I squeaked.

"BOING-BOING!" Og chimed in.

The tadpoles didn't make a sound, of course.

The stranger was much shorter than Aldo and he didn't have that nice, furry mustache that Aldo has. But he did have rusty-colored hair and a rusty-colored beard to match.

He pulled in the cart and looked around the room. "Nice and neat," he said.

That was true. Mrs. Brisbane's room was always nice and always neat.

Then he saw our table by the windowsill. "Oh!" he said. "Aldo left me a note about you."

As he walked toward our table, I squeaked, "Where is Aldo? And who are you?"

He fumbled around in his pocket and pulled out a carrot stick. "Aldo told me to give the hamster a treat—I guess that's you."

"Of course it's me," I squeaked. "Does anyone else around here look like a hamster?"

He pushed the carrot stick between the bars of my cage.

"Thank you," I said, even though I had no idea who this person was.

The man scratched his head and looked around. "He said to give the frog something." Luckily, he spotted the jar of Froggy Fish Sticks. "Ah!" he said. He opened the jar, took out a few sticks and threw them into Og's tank.

"BOING-BOING!" my froggy friend said.

The man scratched his head again as he stared at the tadpoles. "He didn't tell me what to do about you." He leaned in closer to look at them. "Whatever you are."

I understood his confusion. "Who are *you*?" I squeaked.

"Sorry I don't know the ropes," the man said. "I'm just filling in for Aldo! His wife had twins. A boy and a girl."

"YAY-YAY-YAY!" I squeaked. "Did you hear that, Og?"

"BOING-BOING-BOING!" Og replied.

The man smiled. "Aldo said you guys have a lot of personality."

Aldo has a lot of personality, too. I tried to picture a baby girl who looked like his wife, Maria. And a son who looked like Aldo. Did *he* have a mustache like his dad?

The man took his broom and began to sweep the floor. He didn't do the funny things Aldo did—like balancing a broom on one finger. But he swept and dusted, straightened the tables and worked very hard.

"I'm telling you—even if you can't understand me—I really need this job," he said.

"But it's Aldo's job!" I squeaked.

I was happy when Og agreed. "BOING-BOING!"

"He's about to graduate from college, and if he gets a

teaching job, I hope I can move up to being a full-time custodian," he said. "Right now, I just fill in when someone can't make it."

He stopped talking, but I kept listening. After a while, he spoke again.

"I have a wife and kids, too," he said. "The store where I worked closed down, and I've only been able to find part-time work." He stopped and looked over at us. "Hey, why am I talking to a hamster and a frog?"

"Because we're listening!" I squeaked.

"BOING!" Og said.

The room looked fresh and shiny as the man stopped and leaned on his broom. "I'd do anything to get this job," he said. "As long as Aldo has a better job. He's a good guy."

"The BEST-BEST-BEST!" I agreed.

The man was finished, but as he pulled his cart toward the door, he said, "My name is Bob. And I hope I see you again."

He switched off the light and I sat there in the dark for a long, long time.

"Og, Aldo wants to be a teacher," I squeaked. "And I want what Aldo wants. But what will it be like when he's not here every night?"

Og leaped into the water side of his tank and splashed around.

"If Aldo can't be here every night, I hope Bob gets the job," I said.

Then I moved toward the window and looked up at the moon. "I'll miss Aldo so much," I squeaked. "But Bob needs a job, too. And he did give us treats."

"BOING-BOING!"

I was glad that Og agreed with me.

HUMPHREY'S SPRING THINGS
I'm happy for Aldo—he's my friend.
But I'd hate to see the good times end!

Family Matters

The next morning, my classmates ran over to our table to check on the tadpoles—and they didn't even say "good morning" to me.

To squeak the truth, I was trying *not* to look at the tadpoles.

"Look!" Simon shouted as he raced to our table. "Wow!"

I couldn't help it. I hurried to the side of my cage to look at my neighbors. There they were, swimming around their aquarium. Their heads and legs had changed overnight.

They didn't exactly look like frogs, but they were definitely not specks anymore.

My friends all crowded around the aquarium.

Joey opened his notebook and began to sketch.

When Cassie arrived, her cheeks were pink and her eyes sparkled. "I can't believe it! I found another nest in the front yard and it has four eggs in it!"

Everyone gathered around her to see a photo she'd taken.

"Awwww!" they said. And, "They're so cute."

"I'm calling the first eggs Eeny, Meeny and Moe," Cassie said. "Now I have to think of four more names."

"We still need to give the tadpoles names," Helpful-Holly said.

"How about Nog and, um, Yog? After their Uncle Og," Daniel suggested.

Og leaped up and twanged, "BOING-BOING!"

My friends giggled, but I didn't see what was so funny.

"How about Dippy?" Kelsey said. "Dippy and Lippy. Dippy and Hippy."

Thomas shook his head. "Those aren't good names. I still think they should be Tad and Pole."

No one else liked that idea.

"Max," Simon said. "Max and, um . . ."

"Mickey," Tall-Paul said. "Max and Mickey."

Rosie frowned. "What makes you think they're boys? One of them might be a girl."

"*Both* of them might be girls," Nicole said.

They argued—in a friendly way—and finally Rosie said, "Flip and Flap. That doesn't sound like boys *or* girls."

I liked those names. And so did my friends.

"Welcome to Room Twenty-six, Flip and Flap," Mrs. Brisbane said. "Now, students, please take your seats."

We started the day by reviewing my classmates' family trees. It was fascinating to hear the names of my friends' parents. Next, Mrs. Brisbane showed them where to add their grandparents' names.

"Grandma and Grandpa!" Harry said.

Simon grinned. "*Bubbe* and *Zayde*!"

"*Abuela* and *Abuelo*," Felipe said.

Rolling-Rosie gave him a thumbs-up. "Mine, too!"

Goodness, there were so many names for grandmother and grandfather. Poppy and GeeMa. Granny and Gramps. PawPaw and MayMay!

"One thing's for sure," Mrs. Brisbane said. "No matter what you call them, you all love your grandparents. Tonight, please add their real names. First and last. Then we'll add your aunts, uncles and cousins. I'll hand out an example that shows you where to put them."

"I have a lot of cousins," Stop-Talking-Sophie said.

Mrs. Brisbane nodded. "Then you'll have a lot of apples on your tree."

Felipe said, "Let's make Humphrey's family tree!"

The whole class thought that was a good idea, but I wasn't sure I had a family tree. Or even a family.

"Who were Humphrey's mom and dad?" Sophie asked. "Where did he come from?"

Mrs. Brisbane thought for a moment. "Ms. Mac got him at Pet-O-Rama."

I didn't remember my family, but I did remember Pet-O-Rama—and the wonderful day Ms. Mac chose me for the classroom pet in Room 26. Of course, I didn't know she was a substitute for Mrs. Brisbane at the time.

And I didn't know she'd be leaving Longfellow School for a while.

I'm GLAD-GLAD-GLAD she finally came back.

"Humphrey must have had a family," Nicole said.

"I must have!" I agreed.

I remembered Carl and some of the other humans who worked at Pet-O-Rama and took care of us in the small-animal department. But I didn't think of them as family. They never even talked to me!

Mrs. Brisbane said that when humans or animals grow up, they leave their families and go out on their own. "Most of you will move out of your parents' home when you grow up," she said. "But smaller animals grow up faster than humans, so they can leave their mothers much sooner. Does anyone here have a dog that they got as a puppy?"

Some hands went up, including Joey's.

"Dogs are usually adopted by human families when they're puppies. How long does it take for a puppy to be ready to leave its mother?" she asked.

Joey said, "Skipper was about eight weeks old. He wasn't grown up until he was about a year old. But he still acts like a puppy sometimes."

"So it only takes a year for a dog to grow up," our teacher continued. "And it takes an even shorter time for hamsters to be ready to leave their families."

"That's sad," Rosie said.

"Not really," Mrs. Brisbane said. "It's natural. And if

112

Humphrey stayed with his mother or Skipper stayed with his dog family, we wouldn't be able to have them as pets."

Mrs. Brisbane was right as usual. If I had stayed with my family—or even stayed at Pet-O-Rama—I wouldn't have the job of a classroom pet. It's the BEST-BEST-BEST job in the world!

Cassie glanced over at our table. "I guess Og doesn't remember his family. After all, tadpoles are on their own from the very beginning," she said.

"Og looks sad," Rosie said.

"I think he looks as if he's smiling," Mrs. Brisbane said. "Look at his mouth."

I wasn't sure, but my friends chuckled and soon the subject changed.

When Mrs. Brisbane announced another math quiz, I scurried to the front of my cage and looked at Cassie. As usual, she looked worried.

When she glanced over at my cage, I immediately hopped on my wheel and began to SPIN-SPIN-SPIN! Cassie stared at me, and then she closed her eyes and took some deep, long breaths.

Mrs. Brisbane passed out the test papers.

Cassie took a few more deep breaths.

I hopped off my wheel and watched her carefully. She didn't stare at her paper. She didn't hold her stomach.

Cassie picked up her pencil and began to read the questions. She stopped every now and then to take a good, long breath. And then she wrote down her answers.

She looked over at my cage from time to time and I tried to be encouraging.

"You can do it, Cassie!" I said. "You don't have to be perfect—just do your best."

Cassie finished the test before most of my other classmates. When she was finished, she sat back in her chair and smiled.

I was smiling, too, though I'm pretty sure no one else knew it.

On her way out of the classroom for lunch, Mrs. Brisbane asked Cassie how the math quiz went.

"I think I did pretty well," Cassie said. "And my stomach didn't hurt."

~·~

At the end of the day, Mrs. Brisbane made an announcement. "I think some of you know Aldo Amato, our nighttime custodian," she said. "He's Richie Rinaldi's uncle."

"Yay, Richie!" I squeaked. He was one of my friends from last year's class.

"Aldo's wife just gave birth to twins," Mrs. Brisbane continued with a smile. "A boy and a girl. The boy is named Marco, after Aldo's father. The girl is named Anna, after Maria's mother."

My friends began to clap.

Marco and Anna! I didn't clap my paws, but I loudly squeaked, "YES-YES-YES!"

114

As they filed out of Room 26, I heard my classmates buzzing about the new babies. They were as excited as I was.

As soon as the classroom was empty, I jiggled the lock-that-doesn't-lock and scurried over to Og's tank.

"Marco and Anna!" I squeaked. "A boy and a girl!"

"BOING!" he replied.

Then I glanced over at Flip and Flap, swimming in their aquarium. They were also twins.

I'd almost forgotten that Aldo was my old pal Richie's uncle. Was Og really an uncle, too?

Suddenly, it seemed as if everybody in the world had a family . . . except me.

⌒⌒

I wasn't sure whether Aldo would be coming in to clean that night or if it would be Bob or some other stranger. But I wanted to make sure Gigi knew about the twins, so I took a chance and slid down the table leg and raced out of Room 26.

Gigi was still awake when I made my way up to her cage.

"I'm glad you came, Humphrey," she said softly.

"I wanted to tell you that Aldo's wife, Maria, had twins. A boy and a girl!" I said.

"Twins?" Gigi seemed confused.

I explained that when humans have two babies at the same time, they're called twins.

"Oh," Gigi said. "That's very good news."

"And that guy who came in to clean last night, he's just filling in for Aldo," I said.

"Oh," Gigi repeated. "I was a little scared when he came, but he was nice."

"I'm sure Aldo will be back tonight," I said.

Gigi moved a little closer to me. "Humphrey, I'm worried about something."

"What's wrong?" I asked.

"For the circus night, Ms. Mac told us that our booth is called the Clown Toss. Are people really going to throw clowns? That doesn't sound very nice!" she said.

It didn't sound nice at all. Throwing things at people—or animals—isn't nice at all. Especially if the people are funny and like to make people laugh, like clowns.

"I think she might have been joking," I said. "Or maybe you misunderstood what she said."

Gigi nodded. "I hope so. And something else—the children want me to wear a clown hat. But guinea pigs don't like to wear clothes!"

"Neither do hamsters," I said. "I think that's because we're already wearing our fur coats."

Gigi giggled. "You always make me feel better, Humphrey!"

～◦～

I was GLAD-GLAD-GLAD I'd made Gigi feel better. But I didn't feel so great myself when the door opened later that night. I was looking forward to congratulating Aldo, but instead, Bob was back.

116

"Me again," he said as he pulled his cart through the door.

"HI-HI-HI," I said.

Even though I was disappointed, I didn't want to hurt Bob's feelings.

He dusted for a while, and he remembered to give Og and me our treats.

"I told my kids about you," he said. "Now they want a hamster and a frog, too."

"BOING!" Og sounded pleased.

Bob was an unsqueakably nice human, but I still missed Aldo.

I wondered whether he was ever coming back to Room 26. And if not, why hadn't he at least told us good-bye?

～✦～

That night, I had a dream. I don't remember it very clearly, but there was a large, soft, furry creature who smelled wonderful. And I was snuggled up against this creature, along with some other small bits of fur.

I felt so peaceful next to her. And I heard her say something to me.

"Remember this," she squeaked. "No matter where you go, you'll always be my special golden boy."

I woke up with a start and squeaked, "Mother?"

The only answer was Og's loud "BOING!"

"Sorry," I told him. "I think I had a dream about my mother. And some brothers and sisters, too."

"BOING?" Og replied.

I didn't tell him the rest of my dream. After all, he probably didn't remember his mother and father at all.

And he was green . . . not a golden boy, like me.

HUMPHREY'S SPRING THINGS

I felt a little sad to see
No branches on my family tree.

13

Step Right Up!

~·~·~·~·~·~·~·~·~·~·~·~·~·~·~·~·~·~·~

"Let's get our act together," Mrs. Brisbane said the next morning. "We need to make our final plan for Family Fun Night. Here is a list of what some of the other classes are doing."

Then she read from a sheet of paper:

- Clown toss game
- Pizza booth
- Juice and water booth
- Circus crafts
- Tightrope walk on the balance beam
- Popcorn and cotton candy
- Elephant rings
- Circus twirler craft
- Ticket booth
- Hula hoop competition
- Face painting
- Balloon animals

She stopped reading and looked up. "We need to tell Mrs. Wright exactly what we're doing."

"Eeek!" I squeaked.

Was Ms. Mac's class really going to toss clowns? Wouldn't rings for elephants be large? And balloon animals were bound to pop and make a lot of noise.

I wasn't the only one in Room 26 who was confused.

"Are they really tossing clowns?" Daniel asked.

Mrs. Brisbane smiled. "No, of course not. They have a big board painted with clown faces. There are openings where the mouths are, and people throw bean bags to see if they can get them through the clowns' mouths. No actual clowns will be harmed."

My friends laughed and I was relieved, to say the least!

Helpful-Holly waved her hand and our teacher called on her. "What are elephant rings?"

"They're this big!" Felipe held his arms wide apart.

"No." Mrs. Brisbane laughed. "It's a ring-toss game. You have to throw the ring and get it on an elephant's tusk."

"A real elephant?" Cassie looked VERY-VERY-VERY nervous.

"No, I think they're made of clay," Mrs. Brisbane explained. "And they're not quite as big as real elephants." Then she asked us if we were ready to go ahead with the maze and leapfrog games.

"I guess so," Thomas said. "If we can't do the tightrope walking."

"We could have a hamster toss," Nicole suggested.

Just-Joey raised his hand. "I liked the idea of a hamster obstacle course."

Most of my friends nodded in agreement.

"I liked the idea of the leapfrog game," Sophie said. "And of the adults competing against their kids."

Most of my friends nodded again.

"BOING-BOING!" Og said.

"Very well," Mrs. Brisbane said. "Simon's mother has kindly offered to head up a parents' group to build what we need."

"She's a really good artist," Simon said, and Mrs. Brisbane nodded.

"I'm sending a note home to your parents explaining the whole thing," she said. "Oh, and if your dad would like to juggle for us, Sophie, that would be wonderful. But no knives. I think Mrs. Wright would faint."

Sophie looked as proud as Simon did.

"May I be the ringmistress?" Rolling-Rosie asked.

"Oh, I want to be a ringmaster, too!" Felipe said.

"I'll tell you what," Mrs. Brisbane said. "I'll make up a list of jobs and then we'll draw names for them. It's a long evening, so we'll need several ringmasters and other helpers."

But will there be a job for Og and me?

◦◦◦◦

Friday morning, Hurry-Up-Harry came into the room complaining. "It's been raining cats and dogs for two days!"

"Eeek!" I squeaked, and glanced out the window. I didn't see any cats and dogs, thank goodness.

Mrs. Brisbane reminded him that rain in the springtime is very good for green and growing things. "You know the saying: 'April showers bring May flowers.'"

Harry groaned. "The way it's raining, those flowers are going to drown."

It was still raining when Simon's mom came to pick us up.

I hadn't gone home with Slow-Down-Simon before, but I had been to his house. His older sister, Stop-Giggling-Gail, had been in last year's class.

"Slow down," Mrs. Morgenstern said as her son rushed out of Room 26 with my cage. "Poor Humphrey will think he's on a roller coaster."

I've never been on a roller coaster, but it can't be much worse than sliding around my cage like that!

Simon slowed down, but my tummy was still a bit queasy and uneasy.

Gail met us at the car. "Hi, Humphrey!" she said. "Oh, I've missed you!"

"I miss you and your classmates, too!" I squeaked.

On the way home, Mrs. Morgenstern explained that she had started on the signs for our booth. She said some of the other students and their parents were coming over to help out.

"But it's *raining*," Simon groaned.

Gail giggled. "They're working out on the back porch. It has a roof. Besides, it's not going to rain forever."

It was still raining on Saturday, but lots of people showed up to help. Of course, they were on the back porch and I was in Simon's room. I was still unsqueakably curious about what everyone was doing.

I dozed off after a while and was dreaming about my friends from Mrs. Brisbane's previous class. The dream was so clear, I could almost hear A.J.'s booming voice say, "Hi, Humphrey Dumpty!" That was my first nickname, before the Humster.

I heard Gail giggling. Maybe this wasn't a dream after all.

I opened my eyes and poked my head out of my sleeping hut. And there they were: Garth and A.J., Heidi, Sayeh and Gail!

At the beginning of the school year, they used to stop by and say hello to Og and me. But as the year went on, I saw them less and less.

They all leaned down and smiled at me.

"Come on out, Humphrey," Speak-Up-Sayeh said softly.

I raced out of my hut. "HI-HI-HI, old friends!" I squeaked loudly.

Gail wasn't the only one who giggled.

"I remember when Ms. Mac first adopted Humphrey and brought him to Room Twenty-six," Garth said.

123

Now I understood. I was adopted by nice people, just like Thomas!

"I remember when Mrs. Brisbane came back," Heidi said.

I remembered that really well because she wasn't too sure about having a classroom hamster back then.

Gail and her friends settled in on the bed and chairs and talked about me.

"My whole family loves Humphrey," Sayeh said. "He's so funny!"

"Mine, too," A.J. said. "We wanted to keep him."

They all agreed that they'd like to have me as a family pet.

"But Humphrey belongs to us all," Heidi said. "And the kids in Room Twenty-six now."

"Yeah! He has a really big family," Gail said. "All of us!"

Later in the afternoon, the parents took a break and came in to say hi to me.

Heidi's mom, Mrs. Hopper, said, "I understand our favorite hamster is here! Hi, Humphrey!"

"Thanks," I said. I didn't tell her she had purple paint on her cheek.

"You're going to love your booth," she added.

Sophie's dad gave me a huge smile. "Poor Humphrey didn't get much sleep at our house because baby Timothy was teething. He'll have to come back again."

"Anytime!" I squeaked.

Garth rushed in to check on me. "What's going on?" he asked when he saw all the people gathered around.

"We're just visiting Humphrey Dumpty," A.J. said.

"He has a new nickname now," Simon told A.J. "We call him the Humster!"

"The Humster?" A.J. thought for a few seconds. "I like it!"

I liked all of my nicknames and all the students and all the parents.

It's nice to be in such a great, big family!

❧

Late in the afternoon, everybody gathered in the kitchen. Lucky for me, Gail brought me along! Mrs. Morgenstern announced, "We all did such a fabulous job today, we're going to get cleaned up and go out for pizza. On Thursday morning, Daniel's dad will bring a truck to pick up everything and take it to school so we can set up."

"Yay!" Gail said. "Can Humphrey come for pizza, too?"

"Very funny," her mom said.

I didn't think it was funny at all. I would LOVE-LOVE-LOVE to go out for pizza—even pizza with mushrooms on it.

Once I was alone in the house, I started thinking about all the work they'd done on the booth. "*Your* booth," Heidi's mom had said.

My curiosity grew and grew and grew some more.

I wasn't sure what the back porch looked like or where it was, but I decided to take a chance and find it.

I jiggled the lock-that-doesn't-lock and scampered through the doorway. This room had a couch and TV and bookshelves.

It also had a big glass door. I was unsqueakably disappointed that it was the kind of door that slides, because it was impossible for me to crawl under it. But if I stood very tall on my tippy toes, I could see the back porch.

And what I saw made my whiskers wiggle. Wow!

There were stacks of tall boxes painted bright colors and a very tall board painted with red and white stripes to look like a circus tent. A doorway was cut in the middle of the board, and over the opening, painted in big red letters, were the words:

Brisbane's Amazing Animal Acts

Alongside the doorway was another sign.

Do you dare to try
the Humster's Jungle Maze?

The Humster? That's me! And what do you know— my picture was on the sign. I sure wanted to try that maze, but I knew I'd probably never get the chance.

There was one with Og's picture, too. It said:

Take Og's
Frog Leap Challenge!

And there were lots of gray elephant heads on the floor.

The porch had windows on three sides, and I could see that the rain had stopped and the sun was low in the sky.

Everything looked fresh and green and brand-new.

I was about to return to the kitchen when I saw something in the sky that I'd never seen before.

"A rainbow!" I squeaked out loud.

It was just like I'd seen in pictures: a magical arch of many colors across the sky.

"WOW-WOW-WOW," I said.

When the rainbow started to fade, it was getting dark, and I realized that the Morgensterns would be home soon.

I raced back to the kitchen and pulled myself up to the counter, using the handles on the cabinet drawers.

It was unsqueakably hard, but I'm one strong hamster. Kind of like the strong man at the circus.

I ran into my cage and closed the door behind me.

Seconds later, I heard the family returning.

Simon burst into the kitchen and shouted, "Humphrey, we saw a rainbow! I'm sorry you missed it."

"Not a problem," I said as I burrowed into my bedding and quickly fell asleep.

HUMPHREY'S SPRING THINGS
The circus games were ready to go,
But nothing could top a spring rainbow!

On with the Show

I'm always HAPPY-HAPPY-HAPPY to get back to Room 26, but that Monday, I was even more excited than usual. I wanted to tell Og about the circus decorations and the rainbow! I hoped maybe he'd seen it, too.

But as soon as Simon put my cage on the table, Og began to leap up and down. "BOING-BOING-BOING!" he said.

He leaped so high, I thought he was going to pop the top of his tank.

"Goodness," Mrs. Brisbane said. "What is going on with Og?"

Simon was still standing near us, and he gasped loudly. "Mrs. Brisbane, come here quick!" He was staring at the tadpoles.

Mrs. Brisbane gasped, too, when she joined him. "Oh, my!" she said.

"BOING!!" Og twanged.

"Their heads are so much bigger," our teacher said.

"And look." Simon pointed. "Their bodies are much longer. Their tails, too."

"BOING-BOING-BOING-BOING!" Og repeated.

"All right, Uncle Og," Simon said. "We see what happened."

Other students came into the classroom and gathered around.

"Flip and Flap look more like frogs," Rosie said.

"Right on schedule," Just-Joey said. "According to the booklet, it won't be long now before they're real frogs."

I wished my friends weren't all crowded around the tank, because I couldn't get a good look at the tadpoles.

"A-MAZ-ING!" Tell-the-Truth-Thomas said.

"BOING!" Og agreed.

Mrs. Brisbane turned to her students. "Speaking of amazing things, did any of you see the rainbow on Saturday?"

"YES-YES-YES!" I squeaked.

"BOING!" I guess Og had seen it, too. And so had almost all of my friends.

Mrs. Brisbane had planned to start the day with math, but instead, she sent the class to the library to look up facts about rainbows and tadpoles. It takes a really great teacher to change her plans when her students get excited about something.

When they returned, they shared what they had learned.

According to Helpful-Holly, rainbows are caused by light bouncing off water droplets. That's where the rain part comes in.

And Small-Paul explained that the colors of the rainbow are in this order: red, orange, yellow, green, blue, indigo and violet. I wished I'd paid more attention.

"That's Roy G. Biv!" Nicole shouted.

Paul nodded and said, "The letters of his name stand for the colors of the rainbow."

I think every time I see a rainbow from now on, I'll think of Roy G. Biv.

Joey talked more about tadpole development. Some tadpoles take even longer to grow into frogs than Flip and Flap.

Our principal, Mr. Morales, visited our classroom to see the tadpoles. He was wearing a tie with small, colorful rainbows on it.

"I wish my children could see the tadpoles," he said.

"What about seeing us?" I squeaked.

"BOING!" Og agreed.

"That reminds me of something," Mrs. Brisbane said. "The students would like to have Humphrey and Og at their booth on Thursday. As long as it's all right with you."

"Of course!" he said. "I'll bring Willy and Brenda along to see them."

⌣‿⌣

It was one of the busiest weeks I've ever known in Room 26.

One day, Mrs. Brisbane showed the class the list of jobs for Family Fun Night. There would be ringmasters and ringmistresses, ticket takers, prize givers, and students to help people through the maze and run the leapfrog competition.

Then she went down the list and drew students' names out of a big top hat. The hat was the same one that the ringmasters and ringmistresses would wear.

Felipe, Kelsey and Nicole were excited to run the leapfrog game.

Rosie, Daniel, Holly and Tall-Paul would help at the hamster maze.

Joey, Rosie, Sophie, Thomas and Cassie were going to be ringmasters and ringmistresses. Their job was to attract people into the animal acts area.

The rest of the students were ticket takers and prize presenters.

All of my classmates looked happy with their assignments, except for one.

Cassie just stared at the floor and looked a little bit sick.

When my friends left for recess, she stopped to ask Mrs. Brisbane if she could switch jobs and be a ticket taker.

"Why?" Mrs. Brisbane asked.

Cassie held her stomach. "I don't like to talk in front of people. Especially people I don't know."

Mrs. Brisbane nodded. "This isn't like giving a speech. You just stand there and say, 'Step right up to the greatest animal show on earth!' You can do that!"

Cassie didn't look up. "I'm not sure."

"You won't know until you try it," Mrs. Brisbane said. "Remember the ideas we've shared about breathing and positive thoughts."

Cassie nodded.

"This would be a wonderful way to practice those ideas," Mrs. Brisbane said. "Let's try it now. Take some good, deep breaths and tell yourself that you will do a great job."

I was unsqueakably happy to see Cassie use her deep breathing.

"Now say, 'Welcome to Brisbane's Amazing Animal Acts! Step right up and try the Humster's Jungle Maze! Come try Og's Frog Leap Challenge!'"

I LOVED-LOVED-LOVED Mrs. Brisbane's dramatic voice.

Cassie said, "That was great."

Mrs. Brisbane asked her to try it.

Cassie took a good, long breath. "Welcome to Amazing Brisbane's Acts. Um . . . step right up for the . . . um, Humster's . . . um . . . Maze! And Og's Frog . . . Leap!"

Mrs. Brisbane smiled. "That was very good, Cassie," she said. "I know you can do it with a little practice. Give it all you've got."

I hopped on my wheel and started to spin. "You can do it, Cassie!" I squeaked.

Cassie laughed. "Look at Humphrey!"

Mrs. Brisbane laughed. "Can you try as hard as Humphrey does?"

Cassie nodded. "I think so."

"That's all I ask of you," Mrs. Brisbane said.

I squeaked in agreement.

~•~

By Thursday, Flip and Flap had changed again. They looked like tiny frogs with very long tails.

"Why are the tails so long?" Holly asked. "Og just has a little stubby tail."

"BOING!" I don't think Og liked having his tail called a stub.

Joey explained that the tadpoles' bodies would grow much bigger. "When they're fully grown, they'll have stubby tails like their uncle Og," he said.

Og dived into the water side of his tank and began to splash loudly.

Just then, Mrs. Wright came into Room 26. "Excuse me for interrupting," she said. "I'm checking to see if you're all set for tonight."

"Everything's under control," Mrs. Brisbane replied.

"I saw your signs about the hamster maze and frog leap. I want to make sure you're not talking about actual hamsters and frogs," Mrs. Wright continued. "They're not allowed in the gym."

My friends moaned and groaned.

Mrs. Wright is very particular about her gym. I don't think she'd allow humans in the gym if she had her way.

"Is there a rule about that?" Mrs. Brisbane asked.

"Absolutely," Mrs. Wright said.

"That's funny," Mrs. Brisbane said. "Mr. Morales told me it was fine."

Mrs. Wright shook her head.

Joey raised his hand. "Humphrey's been in the gym before. He was there after school. And in the holiday program, too."

Mrs. Wright scowled.

"It would mean a lot if you could bend the rules," Mrs. Brisbane said. "They really want to show off Humphrey and Og."

Mrs. Wright was still scowling. She glanced over at our table. "What's in the aquarium?" she asked.

"Tadpoles," Mrs. Brisbane told her.

Mrs. Wright shook her head. "Strictly forbidden," she said. "But the frog and the hamster can come, if they are contained."

My friends cheered loudly.

"THANKS-THANKS-THANKS!" I squeaked, though no one could hear me over the cheering.

"BOING-BOING-BOING-BOING!" Og shouted.

"Three cheers for Mrs. Wright!" Rosie yelled.

She and my classmates cried out, "Hip, hip, hooray! Hip, hip, hooray! Hip, hip, hooray for Mrs. Wright."

I think Mrs. Wright even smiled before she left Room 26.

～✧～

Once school was over and the building seemed empty, I dashed over to visit Gigi.

"Og and I get to come to Family Fun Night!" I told her.

"At first, Mrs. Wright said Ms. Mac couldn't bring

me," Gigi squeaked. "But then she came back and said the principal said I could come, too."

"Hip, hip, hooray for Mr. Morales and for Mrs. Wright!" I cheered.

"Oh, and my friends tried putting a clown hat on me, but I kept shaking it off until they gave up," Gigi said. "Was that bad?"

"NO-NO-NO!" I assured her. "Just because you're a pet doesn't mean you have to do things you're not comfortable doing."

"Thanks," Gigi said with a big yawn. "I hope I can stay awake tonight."

It was getting dark, so I scurried back to Room 26.

I was so unsqueakably excited, I took a long spin on my wheel to calm down. I hoped Cassie was doing some exercise, too.

A little while later, the door opened and Bob turned on the lights.

I liked Bob, but I was a little disappointed. I hadn't seen Aldo for such a long time.

"Good news," he said as he started to sweep. "You two will be seeing a lot more of me. I just got hired to be the permanent nighttime custodian at Longfellow School starting next fall."

"Oh?" I squeaked.

"BOING-BOING," Og twanged.

"Yep," Bob continued. "Aldo got a teaching job! He's happy and I'm happy, too."

I was happy that Aldo's dream came true.

But it broke my heart a little to think that my good friend was leaving.

·~·

The rest of the evening was a great, big, happy blur!

Mr. and Mrs. Brisbane took Og and me to the gym, where my friends and their parents were setting up.

The door to the gym was draped with red and white striped cloth to make it look like a circus tent. Mrs. Wright was already sitting at the ticket booth. The families could buy tickets there and use them for the games and food.

We passed by Ms. Mac's booth. Gigi's cage was sitting on a table in front of the Clown Toss booth. Big, colorful clowns were painted on the backdrop. They had holes where their big mouths were.

"Watch this, Humphrey," Ms. Mac called out as she tossed a bean bag and it went right into a clown's mouth.

"Way to go!" I cheered.

"Humphrey, I don't think there's any way I'll fall asleep tonight," Gigi squeaked.

As we passed by the yummy-smelling popcorn stand, I saw Gail's mom doing face painting and a man twisting balloons to look like animals. (At least they looked like animals if you used your imagination.)

Then we came to a stop and I looked up.

Oh my! It was thrilling to see the tall entrance that said Brisbane's Amazing Animal Acts, especially since I was one of the amazing animals! Simon's mom hammered the last few nails into the jungle maze sign on one side of the entrance. Simon's dad touched up the paint on the frog leap sign on the other side.

"Perfect," Mrs. Brisbane said. "Absolutely perfect!"

"And here are the stars of the show," Simon's mom said, waving at Og and me.

My heart went THUMP-THUMP-THUMP!

"It's showtime," Mrs. Brisbane told us. I peeked through the doorway and saw that the big, colorful boxes were arranged to make a maze. Rolling-Rosie was rolling her way through it.

Next to the maze, I saw a funny sight. Daniel's mom was down on all fours as her son leapfrogged across her back and over her head, landing in front of her.

The gym quickly filled up with families—and noise. In fact, it was so noisy, my whiskers wiggled, my tail twitched and my ears buzzed.

Og's tank and my cage were set on a table by the entrance to the animal acts.

"Seeing you two will help bring people in," Mrs. Brisbane said.

Thomas arrived wearing a big smile and carrying a slice of pizza. "Cheese pizza," he said. "No mushrooms."

Joey was the first ringmaster, and his voice was loud and clear. "Step right up to the most fantastic animal show on earth! Run the amazing Humster maze! Leap like a frog! Step right up!"

Sophie and her dad arrived, and he juggled near the entrance. People stopped to watch as he juggled three

balls . . . and then four. He could even throw them behind his back and keep them in the air forever!

There was so much to see and hear that I didn't notice when Cassie arrived with her mom and dad.

Her parents stopped to say hi to Og and me, but
Cassie just stared at Joey as he loudly invited people to
come inside the tent, where Small-Paul took tickets.

Tall-Paul arrived with his dad *and* his mom. When
Mrs. Brisbane greeted them, Paul said, "I didn't think my
mom could get off work, but when her supervisor heard
about Family Fun Night, he let her switch nights."

I wished I could give his mom's supervisor a great,
big pawshake!

A.J. and his big family all came and tried the games.
His sister DeeLee had a huge smile on her face as she
carried a gigantic pencil. "I won it, Humphrey!" she told
me. "You had to beat the clock to win a prize and I was
the fastest one!"

"GREAT-GREAT-GREAT!" I squeaked.

Soon Mrs. Brisbane told Joey to hand over the top
hat to Cassie.

She looked scared as the crowds of people walked
by, so I hopped on my wheel and started spinning.
Cassie glanced in my direction.

"GO!" I squeaked.

Cassie closed her eyes, took a very deep breath, held
it and let it go. And another one. Then she opened her
eyes and in a loud, clear voice said, "Step right up, ladies

and gentlemen! See the most amazing animal show on . . . earth! Can you beat the Humster's maze? Can you leap like a frog? Step right up to Brisbane's Amazing Animal Acts!"

"Hip, hip, hooray!" I hopped off my wheel and jumped for joy.

"BOING-BOING!" Og said.

Cassie took a few more breaths and started again. Each time she did it, she got better and better. By the end of her turn, she had a huge smile on her face.

I think she wanted to keep going, but when her time was up, she handed her hat to Rosie.

Mr. Morales showed up wearing a tie with happy clown faces on it. He brought his children, Brenda and Willy, to the table. They were a lot taller than the last time I'd seen them.

"Remember Humphrey?" he asked them. "And here is Og the Frog."

They wanted to talk to us more than play games.

But the biggest surprise of the evening was when I looked up and saw Aldo standing by our table, smiling down at Og and me.

"I have missed you, my friends," he said. "But I took off time when the twins were born. You heard about them, right? Anna and Marco—the most beautiful babies on earth! Then I had finals. And then . . . I got a teaching job!"

"Congratulations," I squeaked, even though my heart was breaking a little bit.

"BOING!" Og said.

Mrs. Brisbane came up to say hello to Aldo.

"It's too early to bring the twins to such a noisy event," he said. "But I wanted to come and thank you for that note you left."

"As soon as I heard Miss Loomis was moving away, I thought of you, Aldo," she said. "I knew Longfellow School would be lucky to have you."

"I'm glad Mr. Morales agreed," Aldo said. "I can't wait for school to start." He turned back to Og and me. "And I'm going to come see you every day and bring your treats," he said.

"Yippeee!" I squeaked with joy.

"Did you hear that, Og?" I asked my neighbor after Aldo had left. "Aldo is coming to teach at Longfellow School and we'll see him every day!"

"BOING-BOING-BOING-BOING-BOING!"

Joey raced over. "Og, why are you shouting? Do you miss Flip and Flap?"

"I think he just wants to be heard," Mrs. Brisbane said.

"I made a decision about the tadpoles," Joey told her. "I really want my own frog at home, so I think I'm going to keep Flap as my pet. I want to make a whole book of drawings of him. But I'll leave Flip in Room Twenty-six, if it's okay with you."

"The students will be thrilled," Mrs. Brisbane said with a smile. "There's always room for another pet in Room Twenty-six."

Even though I was unsqueakably tired, later that night I sat and thought about everything that had happened this spring.

I thought about the crocus poking its purple head up through the snow, and other blooming things.

I thought about how two little specks turned into frogs—and now Og was an uncle!

I thought about Aldo's new family and how he was inspired to go back to school and be a GREAT-GREAT-GREAT teacher, like Mrs. Brisbane. His students would be lucky. I was lucky to know him, too.

I thought about Bob, who needed a job and deserved one. Wasn't it wonderful that when Aldo moved on, Bob got his chance for a new start to help his family?

I thought of how Cassie's family wanted to help her calm down . . . and how I helped them all.

I thought about the new family nesting on Cassie's tree and the many apples on my classmates' family trees.

And I thought about the families building booths, playing leapfrog, running the Humster maze and laughing . . . together. Family Fun Night was truly fun.

I thought about my dream about my mother. Even though I grew up fast, she said I was her golden boy.

Her fur was soft and she smelled *so* nice.

I took out my notebook, and by the light of the streetlamp outside my window, I started to draw a tree. On the tree, I drew little round apples. Then I wrote a name on each one. Mrs. Brisbane. Aldo. Just-

Joey. Rolling-Rosie. Stop-Giggling-Gail. Tall-Paul. Small-Paul. Fix-It-Felipe. Ms. Mac. Og the Frog. Gigi.

I kept writing more and more names of all the humans I loved—and who loved me back. Principal Morales. Speak-Up-Sayeh. Hurry-Up-Harry.

It took me a very long time because I think my family is the biggest and best of all!

And then I added two more names: Flip and Flap.

Because even in a big family like mine, there's always room for more.

HUMPHREY'S SPRING THINGS
My family brings me so much joy,
I truly am a golden boy!

Humphrey's Top Ten
Tips for Understanding Families

1. Families come in all shapes and sizes. There is no family that is too big or too small, as long as there are people whom you love and who love you back.

2. When humans—and animals such as hamsters—grow up, they usually move away from their families, but that doesn't mean that they aren't still connected. Family is family.

3. Members of a family care about each other, share with each other, and help each other.

4. Members of your true family don't have to be related to you. They just have to love you.

5. Families may have disagreements and ups and downs, but in the end, they have a bond forever.

6. All creatures have families, from humans to hamsters . . . and even frogs. (Hard to believe, but true!)

7. Family members don't even have to be the same species to love each other. (Humans love hamsters. They even love dogs and cats—which I don't understand, but it's true.)

8. Some families look alike and some look nothing alike, but they all love each other just as much.

9. Family ties are big and strong. Even if family members live far apart, they still love and miss each other.

10. If you haven't given your family members a hug (or a nice, gentle fur stroke) lately—do it! They'll appreciate it!

Ten Questions About Being a Classroom Pet

~~~~~~

Gigi the guinea pig has only been at Longfellow School for a short time. Here, she asks Humphrey to share his experiences of being a popular classroom pet.

1

Gigi: Hi, Humphrey! I'm shy, so I'm still a little nervous about being a new classroom pet. How did you first come to live in Room 26?

Humphrey: I came at the beginning of last school year. Ms. Mac, who is now your teacher, was a substitute teacher in Room 26 then, and she brought me to school. I was soon so busy looking after my classmates that I forgot to be nervous.

2

Gigi: I hope I forget to be nervous, too. Who was your first friend in Room 26 besides Ms. Mac?

Humphrey: All of my fellow students were sooooo welcoming, they felt like friends as soon as I met them. Wait-for-the-Bell-Garth didn't seem friendly for a while, but it turns out he was just jealous because he couldn't bring me home at the time. Anyway, we ended up being GREAT-GREAT-GREAT pals.

3

Gigi: What was your biggest surprise when you first came to Room 26?

Humphrey: There were two surprises. One was Aldo, who came in to clean at night. I didn't expect that! He has that big mustache, which I thought was a piece of fur. Best of all, he was a true friend from the beginning, and I tried to be a true friend to him. The other surprise was that these large and often noisy creatures called humans turned out to be extremely kind, but they also had problems. I am so proud that I could help them out!

4

Gigi: I love Aldo, too! How did you find out that your lock doesn't lock?

Humphrey: To squeak the truth, I knew it didn't lock from the very beginning. I'm a very curious hamster, Gigi. And so when I saw a lovely peanut on the floor of Room 26 and I was all alone, I pushed on the door and jiggled the lock just right and then—it opened! Last year Mrs. Brisbane found out I could escape and she got me a new cage, but I figured out how to open that door, too. Thank goodness!

5

Gigi: Were you scared the first time you went home with a student? I was.

Humphrey: I would have been scared, but I first went home with a lovely girl named Sayeh. She was shy but

VERY-VERY-VERY smart, and she was so happy when Mrs. Brisbane said she could take me home for the weekend, I wasn't worried at all. And when I met her family, I was so busy helping them, I had no time to be scared!

6

Gigi: How did you feel when Mrs. Brisbane came back to Room 26 and Ms. Mac left?

Humphrey: I felt pawsitively awful. My heart sank all the way to my tippy toes. I hadn't realized that Ms. Mac was a substitute for another teacher who would be coming back. And then, Ms. Mac didn't just move next door—she went all the way to a faraway place called Brazil! My heart was broken. I didn't think I'd see her again. I didn't think I'd ever recover. But there were so many other humans to help that over time, I got used to missing her. I came to love Mrs. Brisbane, too. And then, as you know, Ms. Mac came back! Yay!

Gigi: Yay!

7

Gigi: You have a lot of adventures outside of your cage. Which adventure was the most exciting?

Humphrey: Without a doubt, it was the day I sailed alone on a little sailboat on Potter's Pond. I hadn't planned it and I have no one to blame but myself. There I was, being carried by the tide (and yes, there *is* a tide on

Potter's Pond), and I almost went down with the ship. Luckily, I was saved, and when I look back, it was such an exciting day with pirates and treasure and . . . Ms. Mac!

8

Gigi: What is it like to have another classroom pet in the room?

Humphrey: There is no one on earth like Og! When he first came to Room 26, I have admit I was a little jealous. To squeak the truth, I didn't like him very much. He is green and has no fur. He has an enormous mouth and makes that strange sound: BOING! Worst of all, my classmates thought he was great. But over time, he became my BEST-BEST-BEST friend and he has actually saved me more than once!

9

Gigi: Has anything scary happened to you at a student's house? I worry about this a lot.

Humphrey: Here's my advice to you, Gigi: beware of dogs. Especially a dog named Clem, owned by Golden-Miranda, who is one of my favorite friends. Some dogs like Clem have bad breath and sharp teeth. They aren't very smart (that I can tell) but oh, my, they never give up when they have a goal. Clem's goal was to get me, but I defeated him with rubber bands. But it was a very close call!

Gigi: Why do humans want classroom pets, anyway? I've never understood that.

Humphrey: Ms. Mac explained it to me and it makes sense. She said: "You can learn a lot about yourself by taking care of another species." I think she was talking about humans learning about hamsters. But in the end, I learned SO-SO-SO much about humans by helping them. And I wouldn't want another job in the world.

Gigi: Neither would I!

Keep reading for a sneak peek into Humphrey's first Room 26 adventure!

The Return of Mrs. Brisbane

Today was the worst day of my life. Ms. Mac left Room 26 of Longfellow School. For good. And that's bad.

Worse yet, Mrs. Brisbane came back. Until today, I didn't even know there was a Mrs. Brisbane. Lucky me.

Now I want to know: What was Ms. Mac thinking? She must have known that soon she'd be leaving without me. And that Mrs. Brisbane would come back to Room 26 and I'd be stuck with her.

I still like—okay, *love*—Ms. Mac more than any human or hamster on earth, but what was she thinking?

"You can learn a lot about yourself by taking care of another species," she told me on the way home the day she got me. "You'll teach those kids a thing or two."

That's what she was thinking. I don't think she was thinking very clearly.

I'm never going to squeak to her again. Of course, I'll probably never see her again because she's GONE-GONE-GONE—but if she comes back, I'm not even going to look at her.

(I know that last sentence doesn't make sense. It's hard to make sense when your heart is broken.)

On the other hand, until Ms. Mac arrived, I was going nowhere down at Pet-O-Rama. My days were spent sitting around, looking at a bunch of furry things in cages just like mine. We were treated all right: regular meals, clean cages, music piped in all day.

Over the music, Carl, the store clerk, would answer the phone: "Open nine to nine, seven days a week. Corner of Fifth and Alder, next to the Dairy Maid."

Back then, I feared I'd never see Fifth and Alder, much less the Dairy Maid. Sometimes I'd see human eyes and noses (not always as clean as they should be) poking up against the glass. Nothing ever came of it. The children were excited to see me, but the parents usually had other ideas.

"Oh, come see the fishes, Cornelia. So colorful and so much easier to take care of than a hamster," Mama might say.

Or "No, no, Norbert. They have the cutest little puppies over here. After all, a dog is a boy's best friend."

So there we were: hamsters, gerbils, mice and guinea pigs—not nearly as popular as the fish, cats or dogs. I suspected that I'd be spinning my wheel at Pet-O-Rama forever.

But once Ms. Mac carried me out the door a short six weeks ago, my life changed FAST-FAST-FAST. I saw Fifth! I saw Alder! I saw the Dairy Maid with the statue of a cow in an apron outside!

I was dozing when she first came to Pet-O-Rama, as I do during the day because hamsters are more active at night.

"Hello." A warm voice awakened me. When I opened my eyes, I saw a mass of bouncy black curls. A big, happy smile. Huge dark eyes. She smelled of apples. It was love at first sight.

"Aren't you the bright-eyed one?" she asked.

"And might I return the compliment?" I replied. Of course, it came out "Squeak-squeak-squeak," as usual.

Ms. Mac opened up her purse with the big pink and blue flowers on it.

"I'll take him," she told Carl. "He's obviously the most intelligent and handsome hamster you have."

Carl grunted. Then Ms. Mac picked out a respectable cage—okay, not the three-story pagoda I'd had my eye on—but a nice cage.

And soon, amid squeals of encouragement from my friends in the Small Pet Department, from the teeniest white mouse to the lumbering chinchilla, I left Pet-O-Rama with high hopes.

We sped down the street in Ms. Mac's bright yellow car! (She called it a Bug, but I could see it was really a car.) She carried my cage up the stairs to her apartment! We ate apples! We watched TV! She let me run around outside my cage! She gave me my very own name: Humphrey. And she told me all about Room 26, where we'd be going the next morning.

"And since you are an intelligent hamster who is

3

going to school, I have a present for you, Humphrey," she said.

Then she gave me a tiny little notebook and a tiny little pencil. "I got these for you at the doll shop," she explained. She tucked them behind my mirror where no one could see them except me.

"Of course, it might be a while before you learn to read and write," she continued. "But you're smart and I know you'll catch on fast."

Little did she know I could already make out some words from my long, boring days at Pet-O-Rama.

Words like *Chew Toys. Kibble. Pooper-Scoopers.*

Remember, a hamster is grown up at about five weeks old. So if I could learn all the skills I need for life in five weeks, how long could it possibly take to learn to read?

I'll tell you: a week. Yep, in a week I could read and even write a little with the tiny pencil.

In addition to schoolwork, I learned quite a bit about the other students in Room 26. Like Lower-Your-Voice-A.J. and Speak-Up-Sayeh and Wait-for-the-Bell-Garth and Golden-Miranda. (Even after I found out her name is really Miranda Golden, I thought of her as Golden-Miranda because of her long blonde hair. After all, I am a Golden Hamster.)

Yes, life in Room 26 suited me well during the day. My cage had all the comforts a hamster could ask for. I had bars on the window to protect me from my enemies. I had a little sleeping house in one corner where no one

4

could see me or bother me. There was my wheel to spin on, of course, and a lovely pile of nesting material. My mirror came in handy to check my grooming (and to hide my notebook). In one corner, I kept my food. The opposite corner was my bathroom area because hamsters like to keep their poo away from their food. (Who doesn't?) All my needs were taken care of in one convenient cage.

At night, I went home from school with Ms. Mac and we watched TV or listened to music. Sometimes Ms. Mac played her bongo drums. She made a tunnel on the floor so I could race and wiggle to my hamster heart's content.

Oh, the memories of those six weeks with Morgan McNamara. That's her real name, but she told her students to call her Ms. Mac. That's how nice she is. Or was.

On the weekends, Ms. Mac and I had all kinds of adventures. She put me in her shirt pocket (right over her heart!) and took me with her to the laundry room. She had friends over and they laughed and made a fuss over me. She even took me for a bike ride once. I can still feel the wind in my fur!

I didn't have an inkling—until this morning—of the unsqueakable thing she was about to do to me. On the way to work she said, "Humphrey, I hate to tell you, but this is my last day in Room 26 and I'm going to miss you more than you'll ever know."

What was she saying? I hung on to my wheel for dear life!

"You see, it's really Mrs. Brisbane's class. But just before school started, her husband was in an accident, so I took over the class. Today, she's coming back for good."

Good? I could see nothing good in what Ms. Mac was saying.

"Besides, I want to see the world, Humphrey," she told me.

Fine with me. I've thoroughly enjoyed all the world I've seen so far and would go to the ends of the earth with Ms. Mac. But she wasn't finished yet.

"But I can't take you with me."

All hopes dashed. Completely.

"Besides, the kids need you to teach them responsibility. Mrs. Brisbane needs you, too."

⌣

Unfortunately, she didn't tell Mrs. Brisbane that.

Mrs. Brisbane was already in Room 26 when we arrived. She smiled at Ms. Mac and shook her hand.

Then she frowned at me and said, "Is that some kind of . . . *rodent*?"

Ms. Mac gave her the speech about how much kids can learn from taking care of another species.

Mrs. Brisbane looked horrified and said, "*I can't stand rodents!* Take *it* back!"

The *it* she was talking about was *me*.

Ms. Mac didn't bat an eyelash. She put my cage in its usual place next to the window and said the kids were already very attached to me. She attached Dr. Harvey H. Hammer's *Guide to the Care and Feeding of Hamsters* to

6

the cage, along with a chart to make sure I was fed and my cage was cleaned on time.

"The children know what to do. You won't have to do a thing," Ms. Mac said as Mrs. Brisbane glared at me.

Just then, my fellow students came streaming into the room and within half an hour Ms. Mac had said good-bye to everyone, including me.

"I'll never forget you, Humphrey," she whispered. "Don't you forget me, either."

"Not likely. But I don't know if I can ever forgive you," I squeaked.

And then she was gone. Without me.

Mrs. Brisbane didn't even come close to my cage until recess. Then she walked over and said, "Mister, you've got to go."

But she doesn't know my secret: The latch on my cage door doesn't work. It never has. It's the lock-that-doesn't-lock.

So I've got news for Mrs. Brisbane: If I've got to go, it will be when and where *I* decide to go. Not her.

Meanwhile, I'm not turning my back on this woman. Not for a second. If I ever disappear and someone finds this notebook, just check out Mrs. Brisbane. Please!

TIP ONE: Choose your new hamster's home very carefully and make sure it is secure. Hamsters are skillful "escape artists" and once out of their cages they are *very* difficult to find.

Guide to the Care and Feeding of Hamsters, Dr. Harvey H. Hammer

Night Life

For the rest of the day, I felt SAD-SAD-SAD.

"You look sad, Humphrey," Golden-Miranda said when she was cleaning my cage right before lunch.

According to the chart Ms. Mac had left, it was her turn to take care of me, thank goodness. Miranda was the best cage-cleaner and never said "Yuck!"

She put on throwaway gloves, then cleaned my potty corner, changed my bedding, gave me fresh water and finally—oh, joy!—gave me fresh grain, some lettuce and mealworms.

"This will make you happy," she said as she slipped me the special treat she'd brought from home: cauliflower. Naturally, Miranda had good taste. I promptly saved it in my cheek pouch until I could store it in my sleeping house. Hamsters like to stash food for the future.

After my cage was taken care of, I felt well enough to observe Mrs. Brisbane more carefully.

Now, Ms. Mac was tall, wore bright blouses, short skirts and high shoes. She wore bracelets that jingled-jangled. She spoke in a loud voice and waved her arms and walked all around the room when she taught.

Mrs. Brisbane, on the other hand, was short with short gray hair. She wore dark clothes and flat shoes and she didn't jingle-jangle at all. She spoke in a voice just loud enough to hear and sat at her desk or stood at the chalkboard when she taught.

No wonder I was feeling drowsy after lunch. All that nice food and all that soft talking.

"Is that all this hamster does—sleep?" she asked at one point when she glanced over at my cage.

"Well, he's 'turnal," replied Raise-Your-Hand-Heidi Hopper.

"Raise-Your-Hand-Heidi," said Mrs. Brisbane. "What's 'turnal?"

"You know. 'Turnal. He sleeps during the day," said Heidi.

I was wide-awake now. "Nocturnal," I squeaked. "Hamsters are *nocturnal.*"

"Oh, you mean *nocturnal,*" said Mrs. Brisbane, almost as if she had understood me. She turned and wrote the word on the board. "Can anyone else name an animal that's nocturnal?"

"Owl," said Heidi.

"Raise-Your-Hand-Heidi," said Mrs. Brisbane. "But that is correct. An owl is nocturnal. Anyone else?"

A voice shouted out, "My dad!"

Mrs. Brisbane looked around. "Who said that?"

"He did. A.J." Garth Tugwell pointed at A.J.

Both boys sat at the table nearest to my cage.

"What about your dad?" Mrs. Brisbane asked.

A.J. squirmed in his seat. "Well, my mom always says my dad is nocturnal 'cause he stays up so late watching TV."

Stop-Giggling-Gail and a few other students snickered. Mrs. Brisbane didn't crack a smile.

"Her use of the word is correct," she said. "Though, technically, humans are not nocturnal. Any others?"

Eventually, the class came up with more names of nocturnal animals, like bats and coyotes and opossums, and Mrs. Brisbane said that the class would be learning more about animal habits later in the year.

If she'd just look at me, she could learn a lot. But I noticed for the rest of the day that Mrs. Brisbane stayed far away from my cage, as if I had a disease or something.

She read a mighty fine story to us in the afternoon, though. In fact, I couldn't get back to my nap afterward. It was about a scary house and these scratching noises and . . . a ghost! THUMP-THUMP-THUMP, the ghost came down the hall! Oh, I had shivers and quivers.

I have to say, Mrs. Brisbane knows how to read a story. Her voice changed and her eyes got wide and I forgot about her gray hair and her dark suit. To squeak the truth, my fur was on end! The story had a funny ending because it turned out the ghost wasn't a ghost at all. It was an owl!

At the end of the story, everybody laughed. Even Mrs. Brisbane.

I was beginning to think that life with this new teacher wouldn't be so bad. But I changed my mind when the bell rang at the end of the day and all my classmates raced out of the room, leaving me alone with *her*.

She erased the chalkboard and gathered up her papers. I could tell that we'd be going home soon. Suddenly, I began to worry. What if Mrs. Brisbane lived in a scary house with spooky noises and a thumping ghost?

Or, even worse, what if Mrs. Brisbane had a scary pet, like a dog?

My mind was racing as fast as I was spinning my wheel when she finally approached and looked down at me, frowning.

"Well, you're on your own now," she said.

With that, she closed the blinds and walked away. But I heard her mutter "rodent" under her breath.

She left the classroom and closed the door.

She left me alone. All alone in Room 26.

I had never ever been alone before.

As the room slowly grew darker and quieter, I thought back to the happy times at Ms. Mac's apartment. There were always cheery lights on and music and telephone-talking and . . . oh, dear, during the day I never noticed how the clock on the wall ticked off the seconds one by one very loudly.

TICK-TICK-TICK. I was feeling SICK-SICK-SICK.

I wondered if there were any owls around Room 26. Or ghosts.

I tried to pass the time by writing in my notebook about Pet-O-Rama and my days at Ms. Mac's apartment. Writing took my mind off my jittery nerves. But eventually, my writing paw began to ache and I had to stop my scratchings. If only I could roam free, as I had at Ms. Mac's apartment!

Then I remembered the lock-that-doesn't-lock.

It only took a few seconds to jiggle the door open. I skittered across the table. Then, grasping the top of the table leg tightly, I closed my eyes and slid to the ground.

Ah, freedom! I dashed along the shiny floor. I darted between the tables and chairs. I stopped to nibble a peanut underneath Stop-Giggling-Gail's chair. It tasted delicious and made the coolest crunching sound. I chewed and chomped and gnawed and nibbled. And when I stopped . . . I heard the sound.

THUMP-THUMP-THUMP.

Just like the story Mrs. Brisbane had read us.

THUMP-THUMP-THUMP.

Closer and closer down the hall, coming toward Room 26.

Then RATTLE-SCRATCH. RATTLE-SCRATCH.

THUMP-THUMP-THUMP.

Suddenly, I longed for the protective comfort of my cage. I dropped what was left of the peanut and scampered back. But when I got to the table, I thought a terrible thought. I had slid down the smooth, shiny leg, straight down. But how was I going to climb up again?

I flung myself against the table leg, grabbed on and pushed UP-UP-UP. But I had only made a little progress when I began to slide DOWN-DOWN-DOWN. I was right back where I'd started.

The rattling got louder. The sounds weren't coming toward Room 26 anymore. They were coming *in* Room 26.

Just then, I noticed a long cord running down from the blinds. Without hesitation, I leaped up and grabbed the cord and began swinging back and forth. My stomach churned and I wished I'd never touched that peanut. But with each swing, I got a little higher off the ground. As soon as I saw the edge of the table, I closed my eyes and dived toward it.

Whoosh! I slid across the table and scampered into the cage. As I pulled the door behind me, I was suddenly blinded by light.

The something had turned on the lights and was clomping across the floor. It was huge and heavy and coming right toward me.

Just then, my eyes adjusted to the light and I saw the thing. It was a man!

"Well, well, who have we here? A new student!" a voice boomed.

The man was smiling down at me. My, that was a lovely piece of fur across his upper lip. A nice black mustache. He bent down to peer in at me.

"I'm Aldo Amato. And who are you?"

"I'm Humphrey . . . and you scared me half to death!" I told him. But as always, all that came out was "Squeak-squeak-squeak."

Aldo squinted at the sign on my cage.

13

"Oh, you're Humphrey! Hope I didn't scare you half to death!" he said with a laugh.

"I've just come to clean the room. I come every night. But where have you been?" he said. He rolled up a big cart with a bucket and mops and brooms and all kinds of bottles and rags on it.

"Oh, that's right," he replied as if we were having a real conversation. "Mrs. Brisbane came back today. She's a good teacher, you know, Humphrey. Been teaching here a long time. Wish I'd had a good teacher like her. Say . . . do you like music, Humphrey?"

"SQUEAK-SQUEAK-SQUEAK." I tried to tell him I love music almost as much as I love Ms. Mac. Suddenly, a song came blasting out of the radio on his cart and he set to work: sweeping, mopping, moving desks, dusting.

But Aldo Amato didn't just dust and mop. He spun and swayed. He hopped and leaped. He twisted and twirled.

"How do you like the floor show?" Aldo asked me as he grasped the mop like a dancer holding his partner. "Get it? It's a floor show! 'Cause I'm cleaning the floor!"

Then Aldo roared the biggest roar of a laugh I'd ever heard. His big mustache shook so much, I thought it might fall off.

"You like that? I'll show you real talent, Humphrey!" Aldo Amato picked up his broom and very carefully stood it up with the very tip balancing on one out-stretched fingertip. It wiggled from side to side, but Aldo moved with the broom and managed to keep it balanced straight in the air for an amazingly long time. When he was finished, he bowed deeply and said, "What do you think? I'm going to join the circus!" And he roared again.

Then Aldo wiped his forehead with a big bandanna and sat down at the table where A.J. usually sits. "You know what, Humphrey? You're such good company, I think I'll take my dinner break with you. Do you mind?"

"PLEASE-PLEASE-PLEASE," I squeaked.

Aldo pulled his chair right up to my cage.

"Hey, you're a handsome guy . . . like me. Here . . . a little bit of green won't hurt you, will it?" He tore off a piece of lettuce from his sandwich and pushed it through the bars. Of course, I hid it in my cheek pouch.

Aldo chuckled. "Good for you, Humphrey! Always save something for a rainy day."

The two of us shared a very pleasant meal as Aldo told me about how he used to a have a regular job where he worked during the day. But then, his company closed down and he couldn't find a job for a long time. He couldn't even pay the rent when he was lucky enough to get hired here at Longfellow School. He was glad to get the job, but it's lonely working at night because his friends work during the day. They can never get together like they used to.

I tried to squeak to him about all the creatures, like me, that are also nocturnal and Aldo listened.

"I know you're trying to tell me something, Humphrey, but I can't tell what it is. Maybe you're just saying I'm not alone after all, huh?"

15

"Squeak." He understood!

Aldo stood up and threw his trash into the plastic bag on his cart.

"Well, I've got a lot of other rooms to clean, my friend. But I'll be back tomorrow night. Maybe I'll take my dinner break with you again."

Aldo pushed his cart toward the door and reached for the light switch.

"NO-NO-NO!" I squeaked, dreading the thought of being plunged into darkness again.

Aldo stopped. "I hate to leave you in the dark. But if I don't turn off the lights, I could lose my job."

He clomped back across the floor to the window. "Tell you what. I'll leave the blinds open a little. There's a nice light right outside your window."

After he turned off the lights and left, I chomped on the lettuce I'd saved and basked in the warm glow of the streetlight—and my new friendship with Aldo.

TIP TWO: Hamsters are not picky about their food and eat very little. Make sure to feed your pet a wide variety of tasty foods.

Guide to the Care and Feeding of Hamsters, Dr. Harvey H. Hammer

Meet Humphrey!

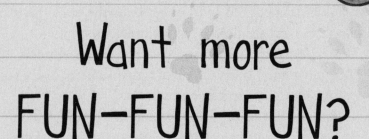

Everyone's favorite
classroom pet!

Want more
FUN-FUN-FUN?

Find fun Humphrey activities
and teachers' guides at
www.penguin.com/humphrey.

Learn more
Humphrey